MW00777430

4

"Well, since Six is so insistent... Sorry, Belial, Astaroth! I'll be sure to bring you two some souvenirs!"

LILITH

One of the Supreme Leaders of the Kisaragi Corporation, known as Lilith the Black. She was happy to be invited by Six. ♪

AGENT SIX'S VIEW
Please send Lady Lilith.
She's super reliable.

THIS VOLUME'S MAIN HEROINE

"Alice, pebble attacks will just force them to hole up in their nest, leaving us without options. We should capture one for observation and figure out their habits."

LILITHIFICATION ① PUT FULL EFFORT INTO TAKING DOWN AN ANTHILL

ALICE KISARAGI
A high-spec android developed with the latest technology the Kisaragi Corporation has to offer. Currently in a rebellious phase.

"Hey, Alice, check this out. You can't flood anthills on this planet."

"Pretty damn impressive for ants. Here, if you survive my pebble attacks, I'll reward you all with sugar cubes."

AGENT SIX

GRIMM
A really, really clingy archbishop.

"... Pretty sure this one's on you, Lady Lilith."

■ GRIMM'S VIEW
What've you two been doing all this time?

LILITHIFICATION ② SAVE THE CITY FROM THE SLIME

"Combat Agent Six, this is our time to shine. Let's shove that troublesome slime back underground. We can worry about finding the culprit once that's done."

CONTENTS

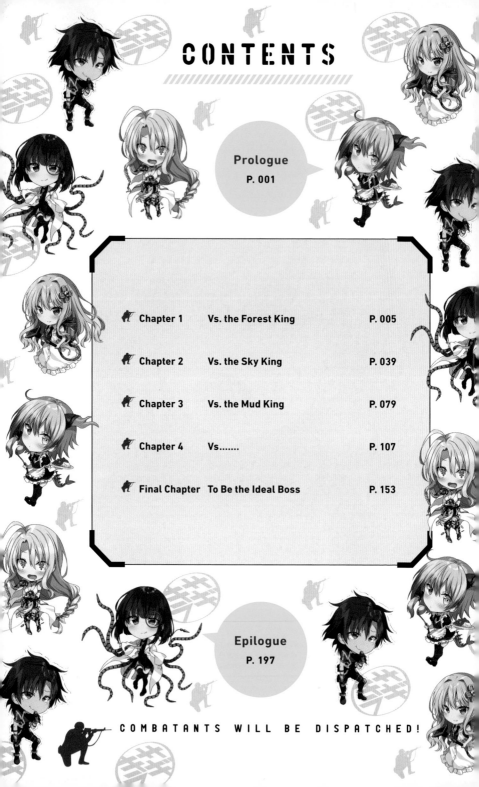

COMBATANTS WILL BE DISPATCHED!

COMBATANTS WILL BE DISPATCHED!

4

Natsume Akatsuki

ILLUSTRATION BY
Kakao Lanthanum

YEN ON

NEW YORK

COMBATANTS WILL BE DISPATCHED!

Natsume Akatsuki ④

Translation by Noboru Akimoto
Cover art by Kakao Lanthanum

SENTOIN, HAKEN SHIMASU! Volume 4
© Natsume Akatsuki, Kakao · Lanthanum 2019
First published in Japan in 2019 by KADOKAWA CORPORATION, Tokyo.
English translation rights arranged with KADOKAWA CORPORATION, Tokyo through
TUTTLE-MORI AGENCY, INC., Tokyo.

English translation © 2020 by Yen Press, LLC

Yen On
150 West 30th Street, 19th Floor
New York, NY 10001

Visit us at yenpress.com
facebook.com/yenpress
twitter.com/yenpress
yenpress.tumblr.com
instagram.com/yenpress

First Yen On Edition: September 2020

Yen On is an imprint of Yen Press, LLC.
The Yen On name and logo are trademarks of Yen Press, LLC.

Library of Congress Cataloging-in-Publication Data
Names: Akatsuki, Natsume, author. | Lanthanum, Kakao, illustrator. | Akimoto, Noboru, translator.
Title: Combatants will be dispatched! / Natsume Akatsuki ; illustration by Kakao Lanthanum ; translation by
    Noboru Akimoto ; cover art by Kakao Lanthanum.
Other titles: Sentoin haken shimasu! English
Description: First Yen On edition. | New York : Yen On, 2019.
Identifiers: LCCN 2019025056 | ISBN 9781975385583 (v. 1 ; trade paperback) |
    ISBN 9781975331528 (v. 2 ; trade paperback) | ISBN 9781975399023 (v. 3 ; trade paperback) |
    ISBN 9781975313685 (v. 4 ; trade paperback)
Subjects: CYAC: Science fiction. | Robots—Fiction.
Classification: LCC PZ7.1.A38 Se 2019 | DDC [Fic]—dc23
LC record available at https://lccn.loc.gov/2019025056

ISBNs: 978-1-9753-1368-5 (paperback)
978-1-9753-1369-2 (ebook)

10 9 8 7 6 5 4 3 2 1

LSC-C

Printed in the United States of America

Prologue

Conference room, Kisaragi headquarters. Astaroth thumbs through some reports as she addresses those assembled.

"Based on the projected timeline, the hideout should be nearing completion."

The reports are marked *Kisaragi Corporation Grace Kingdom Hideout Construction Plan*.

According to this scheme, the Destroyer would pacify the native fauna and allow construction of the frontline base to proceed.

Listening to the report, Lilith nods her head in agreement.

"In that case, it's about time to send over reinforcements..."

"I'll go! Clearly, we need to keep Belial here, given that she's our greatest military asset! Although we've beaten back the heroes, we suffered heavy losses. Given that we're still locked in a standoff and there's no guarantee they'll stay down for long, we should avoid risk and maintain...!"

Belial can't hide a smirk as Astaroth breathlessly rattles off her reasons.

"Don't play coy. It's the bit in the report about him promising himself to someone that's got you all bothered, isn't it? That's why Six always calls you a *tsundere*."

"Don't call me that! Why aren't the two of you more concerned?! Remember, that guy once accepted an invitation from that pink whatever to join the Heroes. Considering that planet's male population has been drastically reduced by the wars, I'm worried he's going to get hooked by some shady floozy..."

"You *do* remember you're an evil Supreme Leader yourself, right?"

"That's beside the point! Anyway, we're in agreement that I'll be the one heading over there, right? In that case, I'll start prepping the reinforcements..."

Just as Astaroth busily begins readying her departure, Belial holds up a hand to stop her.

"Now hold on, Astaroth—I want to go, too. Six and a few others are over there, and more than anything, it sounds like so much fun! Apparently, there are a bunch of mysterious animals..."

"We're sending armed reinforcements, not going on a safari...! Besides, we're still in a cold war with the Heroes...!"

Lilith puts a hold on Astaroth's attempts at persuasion.

"As it happens, I'd like to go, too. Mysterious life-forms, untapped minerals... Given that this planet is full of mysteries waiting to be solved, it's logical that I, the scientist, should lead the reinforcements. Furthermore, our so-called competitors from some undeveloped backwater aren't going to be a match for Kisaragi's technology. It doesn't really matter who we send."

"Whoa, watch what you say, Lilith! When you make fun of opponents and call them things like *backward* and *inferior*, you're pretty much tempting fate! I remember Six warning me about that once!"

Just as the discussion begins to unravel...

"Fine, then let's let Six decide. He can pick who he wants to see most from among us! Er, no! I mean, we'll let him pick who he wants to see lead the reinforcements!"

Astaroth noisily fumbles with her weapons, her expression deathly serious.

""'Did you just say 'who he wants to see'?'""

"Yes! Okay! I said it! So what?! Do you know what the letter Six sent me said?! That he's super popular, that he's gotten engaged, that a loli-girl almost ate him, and that some busty girl kissed him! At first, I thought he was just spouting nonsense as usual, but even Alice's reports are saying similar things! That man's always had a way of drawing in strange women, and I can't even imagine what he's up to now...!"

With Astaroth finally dropping any pretense and going on the offensive, Lilith draws back a hair.

"O-ooookay. So we agree to send whomever Six chooses? ...While Belial's got the whole nurturing persona going for her, I'm guessing he's probably still going to pick Astaroth."

"Y-you think so...? But given that it's *him* we're talking about, he might actually have picked up a local wife... He's pretty absent-minded; he might have even forgotten all about me..."

As Astaroth begins fidgeting and mumbling to herself, Belial grins brightly.

"He's definitely in the meathead category like I am! I wouldn't be surprised if he really has forgotten by now... Wait, wait, I'm kidding, I'm kidding! Cripes! Think about how he wound up joining us in the first place!"

"That's right. Not that I'm proud of it as one of the Supreme Leaders, but Kisaragi's Combat Agents get paid a pittance for some truly awful work. Yet somehow, that gutless Six has stuck with it for all these years. That's all due to..."

Astaroth raises her head, evidently reassured by the two's words.

"Y-you're right... He's constantly tagged along with me all this time, and he put his life on the line for me. I'm sure he'll choose me...!"

Perhaps recalling her past with Six, Astaroth quirks her lips into a slight smile.

Just then, the monitor attached to the teleportation device activates, opening a portal to the planet.

On the screen is the man they've just been talking about.

"Ahem, Combat Agent Six here. The local hideout's done, so I'd like to request reinforcements."

At this long-awaited report, Astaroth turns toward the monitor, a faint flush to her cheeks—

"Hey, Astaroth, did you just loosen your top?"

"...I-it's stuffy in here..."

1

My scream echoes through the park-turned-campsite.

"Goddammitttttt! What the hell is with this planet?! I've had it! I'm going back to Earth!"

It's been a week since the Undead Festival ended and our newly completed hideout exploded in front of our eyes.

This latest setback has put our morale at an all-time low. After all, we've pulled out all the stops for our latest effort—even dragging out the Destroyer—yet this is what we have to show for it.

Sitting on the grass and polishing her shotgun with the occasional *squeak*, Alice opens her mouth to speak.

"An exploding hideout or two is to be expected…but still, this is getting old. We don't even know what caused the blast. We cleared out the area around the base with the Destroyer and burned a decent chunk of the forest for good measure. Just about all we can do is build another base to catch the attacker in the act…"

"Like hell we're doing anything that convoluted! Remember, they won't even send reinforcements until the base is ready. And to think, if we had a Supreme Leader with us, we'd be able to finish off this war with Toris and even do something about our competition and those damned woods…"

The Undead Festival has left its mark on our unit.

For starters, Snow's been focusing on her work as a knight, trying to recover the trust and, more importantly, the pay she lost with her screwups during the Undead Festival.

As I fix my gaze on her bloodshot eyes, showing how hungry and desperate she is for status, I don't see a trace of the proud woman I first met so long ago.

Next, there's Rose. She hasn't been back ever since announcing she'd be spending the rest of her days as Patrasche.

Looks like she's been totally domesticated by a daily routine of eating her fill and being coddled by some old geezer.

Apparently, the only reason she conveniently showed up in the castle courtyard to face off with Gadalkand was because she was there to submit her resignation letter.

I snatched the letter, obviously.

I figured her cover would be blown after the Undead Festival ended and she'd be forced to come back, but I guess I underestimated her dedication.

And finally—

"Hey, Commander, I'm not sure what's got you upset, but I'm sure a full stomach will help. Look! I've got a bento box here that I started prepping before the day even started! I heard you've been living in the park lately, but a bento lunch on the grass should put a positive spin on the situation."

Grimm then happily opens up a bento box, skewering a piece of *karaage* fried chicken with a fork and offering it in my direction.

"Say ah."

Grimm smiles beatifically, despite the bright morning sun she usually withers under.

"...Ah."

I play along and open wide, at which point Grimm pops the piece into her own mouth instead.

"Juuuust kidding. Tee-hee, don't mind me, Commander. It's just a little teasing from your cute subordinate. But if you insist, this time, I'll..."

This seems to amuse her, and Grimm giggles softly while reaching to skewer another piece of chicken...

At the same time, I grab a fork of my own and stab the piece in front of me.

"Oh! No, no, Commander! Let me feed it to you! ...O-oh? Did you want to feed it to me?"

As I wordlessly move the piece of *karaage* toward her, Grimm, with her cheeks flushing, slightly glances off to the side and opens her mouth.

"Ah— F-fwait, fwannder! That's too much! Wait! Did I annoy you?! You're going to get me all greasy! Stop!"

I reduce Grimm to tears by force-feeding her *karaage* without a word. I then confiscate the bento box, munching on what's left while wallowing in despair.

Our assignment is to build a hideout and begin settlement plans.

If we can't find a way to accomplish it, we'll be stuck on this miserable rock for the foreseeable future—

"Screw it, let's call them over anyway."

Ignoring the sobbing Grimm, I realize the obvious as I scarf down the food.

We were told to call over a Supreme Leader after the hideout was completed. They never said anything about the hideout needing to still be there. We *did* actually finish the thing. It's not our fault it blew up almost immediately afterward.

"I spent all night making that lunch! At least pretend you're enjoying it! Or at the very least, stop eating it in silence! One word of praise...that's all I ask..."

Just like that, we're technically finished with our hideout-construction mission.

Sure, it exploded after completion, returning to dust.

I suppose it's a technicality verging on fraud, but as a proper evil minion, this is the sort of thing we're supposed to take pride in, right?

"And another thing, what happened to the necklace or ring you promised to buy me?! I'm not saying this because I want the physical object, mind you. I just want...well, a token of your...love and affection...!"

I finish off the last of the food.

"Yo, Alice, I figured out what we're gonna do next! Technically, we already finished building our hideout. Let's just go ahead and call over one of the Supreme Leaders tomorrow. Then if they ask us where the hideout is, we'll flat-out tell 'em it blew up. Once we get them over here, they'll be stuck for a while. So while we've got 'em, we can get 'em to help us solve our pesky exploding-hideout problem."

"...That's all well and good, but everything depends on who we call over. For example, this sort of stunt's not going to fly with Lady Astaroth."

"You bastard, you're not listening to a word I'm saying! Hrmph! Yes, clearly, it's my fault for bothering with a bento in the first place!"

Alice looks at me skeptically, but I already know who we're calling over.

"...What's going on, Grimm? You look like you're about to cry. Oh, the bento was delicious, by the way. Thanks a bunch."

After spending the past few moments yammering on about

something, Grimm looks over at me. It seems like she has something she wants to say, but she only manages to mumble a few words.

"That's not fair, Commander..."

What's her problem?

2

The next day.

"Please send Lady Lilith."

"Whaaa—?! M-me?!"

As we request reinforcements from Kisaragi headquarters, Lilith's shock echoes from beyond the communications monitor.

Yes, the one I want is Lilith the Black.

The mad scientist who sent me to this planet without any preliminary testing whatsoever.

"Why would you be so surprised, ma'am? You're a scientist, and considering we're on a largely unexplored planet, I figured that'd make you the best candidate."

"Well, sure, I'm the obvious pick if you put it that way! I'm definitely the most logical choice, but still!"

Ordinarily, Lilith is one of those shady characters who could fill a person with dread with a smile alone, but something's off about her today.

"Oh, I wanted to ask. Is something wrong with Lady Astaroth? Things seem a little hectic over there."

"This is all your fault! W-wait, Astaroth! Calm down!"

On the other side of the monitor, a teary-eyed Astaroth grabs Lilith by the shoulders and shakes her back and forth.

Lilith eventually regains her composure and looks up at me through the monitor.

"Six, are you sure I'm the right choice? When it comes to combat, both Astaroth and Belial are stronger than me, and..."

Pulling a stunt this close to a scam on someone as serious as Astaroth would easily land me a one-way ticket to hell. On the other hand, Belial is actually such a sweetheart deep down that I can't bring myself to scam her.

"Well, even Combat Agents like us can go toe-to-toe with the enemy leadership, meaning any of our Supreme Leaders can handle them with ease. We're counting on you, Lady Lilith."

Hearing that, Lilith's expression lights up, and she scratches at the back of her head a bit shyly.

"Well, if you put it that way, Six, I guess I have no choice! Sorry, Belial, Astaroth. You know Six and I are gaming buddies, so that's probably the reason. Mm-hmm. I'm not gloating, honest. I'll bring you two back some really great souvenirs!"

"Say, Six, are you sure you want Lilith? Also, about eighty percent of your letters make no sense; could you clarify...?"

"Six! How ya doin'? We've got some new recruits lately! They go on about weird things like Chosen Ones and Demon Lords—bet you'd get along with them! I'll introduce you when you get back!"

As the three of them crowd the monitor, I can't help but curl my lips into a forced smile at the familiarity of it all.

"I'm glad you all seem to be doing well. For now, this is the Kisaragi Corporation Grace Kingdom branch, eagerly awaiting Lady Lilith's arrival—signing off!"

I straighten my posture and snap off a salute to the monitor.

Ten minutes later.

A voice verging on a scream rings out through the park that's housing our temporary hideout.

"What do you mean, there's no hideout?! Could you run that by me again?!"

The voice belongs to a beautiful girl dressed in a lab coat, her black hair in a bob.

It's the Kisaragi Corporation's antisocial princess, who we were chatting with over the monitor just a few minutes ago.

"We're not exactly living in luxury here, either. I mean, we finished construction on the hideout and ended up back in our tents a day later. Can you get HQ to send us some mobile trailers, at least?"

"Waaaait a minute, tents?! I'm a Supreme Leader! The Kisaragi Corporation controls the majority of Earth, and I'm one of its head honchos! Me, one of the greatest inventors of the age! You expect me to live in a tent?!"

It would have been one thing when Kisaragi was still a poor, little evil start-up. Given that she now lives in a mansion with a swimming pool in the middle of the city, though, Lilith's a little too pampered to accept tent life.

"Tents aren't the worst part of it. Our living conditions here are practically medieval. Like, get this: Some idiot sold off all our toilet paper because it's apparently really valuable here."

The idiot in question is Snow, who's been living in our camp ever since she got evicted for not paying her rent.

"Wha...? Seriously...?! Then what's the toilet situation here? Are there no bidets?!"

"Latrines are more or less standard, but depending on the circumstances, we just dig a hole and bury our business."

Still, Lilith's a battle-hardened Supreme Leader of an evil organization.

Just because she's sampled the sweet taste of luxury doesn't mean she's against some rough living here and there...

"NOOOOOOOO! I'm leaving! I'm going back to Earth! No hideout...that means no AC, right?! No PCs and no video games, no TV, and no Internet?! I'll miss the Sunday episode of *Magical Girl Puikyua!*"

"We don't get broadcasts, so having a TV wouldn't have helped anyway. Could you maybe make do with the fact that we've got real, live Magical Girls here? As for going home, well, without a hideout, there's also no way to use a teleporter to get back to Earth."

The color drains from Lilith, and she freezes.

Wait, I thought she came here as backup. She's acting like she's here on vacation.

"Gaaaaaaaaaahhhhhh, you bastard! I should've known something was up when you specifically asked for me! What a letdown! This is a scam! A SCAM, I TELL YOU!"

...So that's how it's gonna be? Whiny little brat.

"Oh, so you're the victim now, eh, tomboy? If we're talking about scamming, you're the one who started this damned cycle! I haven't forgotten that you zapped me over here without any explanation or so much as a safety test! Oh, right, you were supposed to let me grope you as compensation!"

"Wha...?! W-wait just a minute there, Six. My theories made it clear the teleporter was safe...! And I don't remember promising you that! And I apologized! I already apologized!"

Seeing my sudden anger, Lilith cuts short her whining, backing away from me.

"And then there's all those fake promises you made to encourage me, like stuff about a planet where everyone loves me without question, a planet where the beauty standards make me a stud, or a planet where I'm the only man! And then of course you just neglected to mention that it'd take a month to assemble the teleporter and stabilize the connection!"

"Wh-what? I didn't say anything like that! That wasn't my pitch! ...W-wait...assembling the teleporter and stabilizing the connection...takes a month...?"

The color further drains from Lilith's face, going from blue to paper-white.

Seems she's finally realized her situation.

"That's right. We have to assemble one from scratch, so it'll take at least a month for you to be able to teleport. Therefore, Lady Lilith, no matter how much you cry, no matter how big a tantrum you throw, you still won't be home any earlier than a month from now."

"IDONWANNAAAAAA!! DONWANNNNAAAAAAAA!!"

"H-hey, you're still one of Kisaragi's Supreme Leaders! Please don't pitch a fit out in public. It's embarrassing! I mean, people are starting to stare."

Passersby are starting to glance over at Lilith from off in the distance as she leans against both my arms and sobs hysterically.

Why is it she's so useful when it comes to brainy things but so useless in everyday life?

I'm glad we sent Grimm home before calling in reinforcements.

I can't very well expose a subordinate to one of my bosses throwing a tantrum.

"Now please calm down and send in a request for some trailers. Hell, even basic amenities would be fine now. No doubt you'd like to avoid the tent life, too, right, Lady Lilith?"

"Obviously, I don't wanna live in a tent, but... Six, I won't forget that you lied to me. You're getting court-martialed the moment I get back to Earth."

Lilith stands, taking her device in hand with a sour expression.

"If it comes to that, I'll be sure to take you down with me. Betcha didn't know I'm aware of all the stuff you bought with the money you claimed was for 'research and development.'"

"Six, let's make sure our trailer home is top-of-the-line. And let's get you guys some luxuries. We'll say it's for all the hard work the Combat Agents have put in. How about some top-shelf champagne, huh? Huh?"

"Now that's the sort of quick decision-making we admire you for, Lady Lilith! We Combat Agents will follow you to the ends of this planet!"

As I rub my hands together, Lilith sends her order through her device with a faintly satisfied expression.

"Now, now, Six, flattery will only get you some high-priced champagne and snacks. Heh-heh, just make sure you give me all tens on the next internal survey."

The survey is basically a popularity contest within Kisaragi. It's published each month in the company newsletter and has a ranking of the most admired mutants and Supreme Leaders.

It's supposed to provide encouragement to the ranks, but at the moment, it's just a way for the high-ranked mutants and Supreme Leaders to gain favor in their struggle for dominance.

"Leave it to me. You'll be my pick for Ideal Boss, Most Admired Agent, and Top BILF."

"This is the first I'm hearing of that third category... I'm guessing the *B* in *BILF* stands for *boss*? Who the hell came up with that anyway? You don't need to vote for me for that one... Hmm. Instead of a trailer and champagne, they just sent a piece of paper."

A single sheet of paper arrives in front of Lilith and flutters to the ground.

I lean over to pick it up and read its contents.

"Let's see. 'Trailers are too big to fit into the teleporter, so we can't send them. As for the luxury items expensed to the company, we've been instructed by Lady Astaroth to simply say 'piss off''... Lady Lilith, are you sure you're actually one of the Supreme Leaders?"

"Whhhhhyyyyy?! They were able to disassemble the Destroyer and send it in piece by piece! And don't you think 'piss off' is a little too mean? Geez!" Lilith grabs the paper from my hands, confirming the message before lashing out at me.

"Perhaps it means they consider a trailer nonessential equipment, so it's not worth the time to disassemble like the Destroyer?"

"...B-but I'm one of the Supreme Leaders... I'm still one of the top Supreme Leaders..."

*   *   *

Lilith falls silent in shock, and Alice arrives as I'm trying to cheer her up.

"Yo, Six, how'd it go? We get the things we wanted from Lady Lilith?"

"Oh, hey, Alice. Nope, didn't work, just like you said. Seems Lady Lilith is a lot more useless than I thought."

"Wha—?!"

After hearing my exchange with Alice, Lilith comes out of her trance and sharply glances up.

"Told ya. Lady Lilith's an idiot savant. Unlike the other two Supreme Leaders, I figured most of her requests would get denied."

"Seriously? Didn't know they thought so little of her. What a disappointment! To think I admired her…"

"Hold on just a minute, you two! You're still talking about your superior here!"

Well, I guess, but c'mon.

"Sorry! But I'm an evil minion, after all!"

"Sorry! But I'm an evil android, after all!"

"I know I'm the one who built you that way, but you're REALLY annoying when you say that just like Six!"

Lilith speaks through gritted teeth as the two of us straighten and snap off a salute.

"That's because you used Six's samples for my personality matrix. I've always wanted to chew out Lady Lilith for that!"

Wait…what?

"Whoa, wait, what the hell? That's news to me. When did you take a sample of my brain?"

"Don't be stupid—well, stupid*er* than usual. We wouldn't take samples from your broken brain. That would've just made me an empty-headed moron. But I was constructed to be your support android, which means my personality was designed specifically to match yours by analyzing your actions and personality patterns."

Uh-huh, right. I still don't get it.

"So basically, that means you're tailored to coddle me?"

"Your guess isn't even in the same neighborhood, but let's just go with that. To put it in a way you understand, though, my bad attitude is modeled on yours."

Oh, c'mon…

"Lady Lilith, my attitude's not nearly as bad as Alice's, is it? I'm actually kind of hurt to be told I'm similar to this dry, cynical, and merciless hunk of metal!"

"Yeah? That's my line! Time for a change of sample! Gimme a new one!"

"The more you two talk, the more you sound like a pair of siblings. But you know…"

Seems Lilith's regained her calm as she takes a fresh assessment of her surroundings.

"So this is the alien planet. All those reports you two sent definitely piqued my curiosity. I admit I'm having trouble containing my excitement in spite of myself."

Lilith takes several deep breaths, as though confirming the oxygen levels, and looks around with shimmering eyes.

"It's a little hard buying your whole scientist shtick after watching you bawl like a toddler just minutes ago."

"Q-quiet, Six! This is supposed to be a memorable moment—don't ruin it with your commentary!"

Lilith gazes up at the sky, her cheeks faintly flushed, and begins a long monologue.

"Do you understand how many generations of humanity have gazed up at the stars, dreaming of setting foot on distant new worlds? Have you ever imagined O-Parts so far beyond human technology that they're like magic? Did you cower as a child imagining invasions by people from deep underground, from the sea, or even Mars?"

"Hey, Alice, check this out. You can't flood anthills on this planet.

Watch… When you pour water down them like this, they'll block it with a leaf and start bailing the water out."

"Pretty damn impressive for ants. Here, if you survive my pebble attacks, I'll reward you all with sugar cubes."

As Lilith rambles on, Alice and I turn our attention to poking an anthill. Lilith quickly joins us, squatting down nearby.

"Fascinating…they've got a room filled with leaves to use as a barricade in emergencies. Alice, pebble attacks will just force them to hole up in their nest, leaving us without options. We should capture one for observation and figure out their habits."

"Understood. Let's grab this one; it looks like the strongest."

Anyone else would probably be angry that we'd stopped listening to them, but Lilith's endless curiosity means she's easily distracted by something novel.

That day, after trying to engage in a long, philosophical discussion, Lilith instead acquired three notebooks full of information about attacking anthills, played some cards in a tent, had some of Russell's curry, then happily went to bed.

3

"…What am I doing? At this rate, I'm as big a moron as Six!"

The next morning.

Waking from her slumber, Lilith lets out a shrill screech, storming out of her tent and directing her renewed ire at me.

"Six! Just what are you wasting my humanity-leading intellectual powers on?!"

"Wasn't it fun attacking that anthill? I mean, I sure didn't expect them to stage a counterattack to free our captive. I take my hat off to 'em."

"So true. And to top it off, the moment they realized they couldn't win, they started offering pebbles of an unknown alloy as though trying to pay a ransom for the hostage… No, no, no! I'll admit the anthill attack was fun, but I'm here as a reinforcement!"

Lilith shakes her head, as though remembering what she came to do, and raises her voice.

"You've been a serious help. If it was just Alice and me, they would've holed up in their hill, and…"

"Forget about those ants! First, we get a hideout! Then, we destroy our competition! I mean, without a base of operations, I'll never get home!"

Lilith then glowers at the tents.

"Me, a top Supreme Leader of the great Kisaragi Corporation, reduced to living in a tent! Six! Do you call this an acceptable state of affairs?"

"I dunno; last night, you seemed pretty happy playing cards with us in the tent. You also seemed to be a pretty big fan of the curry."

"That's beside the point! …Oh, speaking of which, let's have a chat with the pretty Chimera who made the curry I had last night. She's currently investigating her past, right? And I remember reading that you recruited her as a Combat Agent in training."

The pretty Chimera who made the curry? Oh, she must mean Russell.

The Chimera who's looking into her past and was recruited to be a Combat Agent in training is Rose, but if she wants to chat with a Chimera, I guess I'll go get Russell.

"What now, Six? I'm kind of busy with everyone's laundry."

"Yo, this lady wishes to speak to you. I wasn't able to introduce you last night, but this is Lady Lilith the Black, one of Kisaragi's top Supreme Leaders."

Hearing her introduced as a top Supreme Leader, Russell twitches and shudders.

"Hello there, pretty Chimera. I see—a little horn, a tail, and mismatched eyes, just as the reports said."

"U-um…h-hello…"

Russell is already on the back foot, evidently because he's already well aware of the strength and abnormality of Kisaragi operatives.

As for Lilith, she's examining Russell as though she's studying a particularly interesting specimen.

"No need to be so tense. So I hear you're interested in learning more about your past?"

"…? U-um, no, I'm not particularly hung up about the past…"

Russell looks nonplussed at Lilith's remark, but she continues:

"Strange, that's what the reports said. How odd. Anyway, on to the next question… How are you holding up? Do you think you'll settle into our organization? Six and the others haven't done anything weird to you, have they?"

Lilith smiles over at the slightly anxious Russell to put him at ease, speaking to him in a gentle tone.

"Weird? I'm not sure, really… Well, I'd like them to stop hiking up my skirt for a peek while I'm working because it's really distracting, but otherwise…"

"Hey, Six? I know we promote acts of villainy, but to sexually harass someone so young…"

Yep, now she's looking at me like I'm worth less than garbage.

"Well, we don't get any Evil Points for peeking, so I doubt Russell minds all that much."

"Really?! B-but…that's ridiculous…"

As Lilith's gaze shifts from disgust to incredulity…

"So long as they don't interrupt my work, I really don't mind having my skirt hiked up. I mean, sure, I do think it's pretty stupid, but whatever."

"You need to value yourself more, pretty Chimera! Is it that you lack a sense of shame because you're a Chimera?! Six, she's too naive—I'm going to put her under my protection!"

Seems like she's operating under a massive misunderstanding.

"Lady Lilith, Russell's a guy."

"Just what the heck are you on?!"

Lilith shoots a look at me with a deadly serious expression.

"Six is right. I'm a guy."

"And what are you going on about, too?"

Since Lilith won't take our word for it, I decide to show her his *indisputable evidence.*

"...Hey, Six, can we wrap this up? I'm getting embarrassed."

"But she'll keep treating me like some pervert otherwise!"

Faced with the hard evidence that Russell is a guy, Lilith slumps to the ground in confusion.

"Is that unique to Chimeras? Are Chimeras intersex? No, no, the reports clearly said the Chimera in Six's group was a girl, so what could have happened in this short time frame? Oh, I get it. She's still a girl at heart. Of course, Kisaragi's a tolerant organization, so employees are free to identify however they feel—"

"Actually, he's dressed in girl's clothes because Tiger Man likes it."

"The world might consider me a genius, but I can't make heads or tails of you lot!"

Lilith hops to her feet, sighing in consternation.

"How am I supposed to report this to the others back on Earth...? That prude Astaroth will have a stroke if she hears Six is hiking up the skirts of cross-dressing boys..."

"Oh yeah? I wonder how she'll react to one of the Supreme Leaders staring at a cross-dressing boy's dick."

"Okay! Let's just keep today's events between us! If I recall correctly, your name's Rose, right, Chimera? Rose, I'm going to give you a little bit of spending money, so forget what's happened today."

Lilith is so flustered that she hands over a wad of cash, completely forgetting that our currency has no value on this world.

"I'm not Rose. I'm Russell."

"Really? REALLY?! What are you trying to get out of teasing me?!"

A short while later, Russell returns to his laundry, and Lilith starts recovering her composure.

"Lady Lilith, would you please stop procrastinating and start getting some actual work done?"

"I wasn't exactly *trying* to procrastinate! Oh, for the love of... Alice! Aliiiice! Come along, it's time for work!"

Lilith calls over Alice, who has been standing off to the side, pretending to be a passerby.

"...I'm afraid I'm busy dropping sugar cubes into the anthill, so do you mind if I stay here?"

"Of course I mind! Alice, have you been hanging around Six so much that you've been infected with his rebelliousness?"

Since arriving on this planet, Lilith has been conspicuously short on patience, but she's still technically one of Kisaragi's top Supreme Leaders, so we need to get her to build the hideout.

"Well, why don't we head out, Lady Lilith? Though elite agents like myself may be struggling with the construction, I'm sure it'll be a snap for you."

"I don't know when you became an elite agent, but leave it to me. I'll show you the true power of Kisaragi technology and a top Supreme Leader!"

4

With Lilith, a top Supreme Leader, on our side, we make our way to the woods.

"Well! Take a look at how clean the roads are, Six! Do you understand that even this little detail is a treasure trove of information?"

Or not.

"Based on the fact that the roads aren't clogged with waste, we can tell the local residents are aware that excrement invites disease. Of course, they might just like cleanliness, but it's possible the standard of medical knowledge here is higher than we think!"

Passing through the city, Lilith's been stopping every few steps to make observations of this sort.

"Either that, or this planet once had a highly advanced civilization, and while the culture itself died out, some of its knowledge has persisted through popular lore—"

I turn to Lilith as she glances around the streets like a kid in a candy store.

"Lady Lilith, I really couldn't care less about this city's poop situation. Can we please leave already? If we don't, your return to Earth will be delayed indefinitely."

"That's right! But still, this is all very fascinating… Oh! Hey, look over there, Six, there's a tank! That must be the one from the reports!"

Seeing the tank just sitting there in the middle of town, Lilith rushes over for a closer look.

"Hey, Alice, mind doing something about that childish creator of yours?"

"She's *your* boss. You've known her longer than I have."

—After finally reaching the city gates by dragging Lilith along, we find a bunch of kids crowding around the Destroyer parked beyond the walls.

Seeing the children, Alice runs toward them.

"You damned brats, don't touch the Destroyer!"

Just like with her shotgun, Alice has grown oddly attached to the Destroyer and evidently can't stand people touching it.

"Who the hell are you calling a brat?! You're smaller than I am!"

"Hey! It's that kid who's always hanging around the Fly! Get outta here!"

"You're right! And the Fly's hanging out back there! Bet she's one of his lackeys! Throw some rocks at 'em!"

The kids don't take Alice very seriously, probably because she looks about their age, which sends her into a frenzy.

"So that's how you want it, you snotty brats? Fine! Get ready to cry!"

Alice catches a rock that was thrown at her, then jumps the tallest boy in the group.

"You're such a *girl*! Why don't you go back to—? Ow! Hey! Ow, ow, ow, ow! Stop it! …Gaaah!"

Alice takes down the boy she tackled, then, grabbing at one of his legs, begins hammering his shin with the rock in her fist.

"Hey, stop it! You made Pikke cry!"

"Okay, okay! We were wrong! We're sorry! So stop it! Please just stop! C'mon, stop it, all right?!"

As Alice continues obsessively attacking the kid's shin, the other boys hurriedly move to stop her.

Lilith stares confusedly at the weirdly immature android.

"Hey, Six, is Alice always like this? Even taking into account the fact that you've been a bad influence on her, picking fights with kids is a pretty good sign she needs some maintenance…"

"Bad influence? She's actually got a shorter temper than me and tends to start fights more often than I do. Wait here a minute, I'm gonna go help her."

"Stop that! And, Alice, that's more than enough; give it a rest—!"

Finally making our way out of the city, we've arrived at our destination despite Lilith curiously inspecting every little thing on the road. The Cursed Forest.

When I first heard the name, I thought they were being a little too melodramatic, but the name just feels appropriate now.

We're still not sure why the completed hideout exploded.

At times like this, the best course of action is to just toss it up the chain for an able boss to handle.

"Lady Lilith, just so we're clear, this forest is really messed up. Please be careful."

"As if some forest is any match for Lilith the Black! If I recall your reports correctly, the problems were monsters, tribes of savages, and natural disasters, right? Then there was the attack on the newly constructed facility that you still haven't been able to identify... Does that about cover it?"

Lilith begins fiddling with her wrist device...

"Best to turn those things into radioactive ash with the purifying fire of thermonuclear—"

...only to be promptly restrained by Alice and me.

5

At the site planned for our base, Lilith sits hugging her knees with a sour expression.

"I'll gladly admit this planet is fascinating, but I want to go home as quickly as possible."

"Hey, I'm looking forward to getting home, too, which is why I'm counting on you. But we need you to work instead of spending all your time pouting."

She may be the crazy boss who wanted to solve the cursed-woods problem using nukes, but Lilith's still one of the more restrained members of the Kisaragi leadership.

"There are definitely times when Lady Lilith acts without thinking. Given that we're looking for new lands to populate due to Earth's various problems, turning our prospective new home into a radioactive wasteland would defeat the purpose, wouldn't it? Stop wasting time and use that stupidly inflated Evil Point total to build us a lair."

"Hey, Alice, you do realize that I'm your creator, right? Your attitude only seems to be getting worse..."

As a Supreme Leader, Lilith's grown accustomed to being surrounded by legions of fawning sycophants. Casual disrespect is an experience totally alien to her. She stands up despite her sour expression.

"Fine, if that's what I need to get back home. I'll show you the power of a Supreme Leader!"

Lilith loudly makes her declaration, throwing open the front of her lab coat.

At that moment, the tentacles the mad scientist implanted into her body come out of hiding, their metal surfaces glinting.

Growing out of her sleeves, hem, and neckline, the eight metal tentacles aim toward the forest, their tips glowing.

"First, let's clear some of that forest and reduce the enemy's territory!"

At her words, a barrage of light lances out toward the woods.

The rays emitted by the tentacles work as advertised, turning the dense woodland into an open clearing.

In the blink of an eye, the forest has been reduced to a charred wasteland past the horizon. That's the level of craziness one can expect from a Supreme Leader.

"Next, we overwhelm them with sheer numbers! I'll import some supplies using my abundance of Evil Points!"

A few minutes after Lilith fiddles with her device, piles of heavy metal plates start arriving on the foundations we laid for our hideout.

The tentacles sprouting out of Lilith then grab the plates, planting them into the exposed earth.

The tip of a tentacle glows brightly with blue-white light, welding them together...

"Lady Lilith, I've always meant to ask. Given how useful those tentacles are, could you put a couple in me, too?"

"These appendages put a really heavy burden on my brain to operate! Just one would overload your synapses, and we'd end up with a terrible tragedy!"

I briefly consider asking her if that's her way of saying she thinks I'm stupid, but even with all her smarts, Lilith herself can only handle eight of them. Bet it really would end tragically for me.

"Let's say you had eight arms, Six. Would you be able to do something different with each arm?"

Taking a closer look at Lilith's tentacles, each is moving independently of the others.

One welds, another hauls metal plates, yet another scratches Lilith's back, while a fourth hands her a bottle of iced tea—

"...It actually looks pretty easy, so yes, I'd like one, too."

"No way! Tentacles are part of my identity! Do you know how hard it was for me to create the mutant Anemone Man?"

The construction proceeds rapidly, making all our struggles seem ridiculous in hindsight.

It was at that moment...

"Oh! Lady Lilith, it's them! The Bashin tribe! Careful! They'll try to drive monsters toward us. You can already see some mokemokes and mipyokopyokos here and there!"

"...Mokemokes and mipyokopyokos? Really? Alice, can't you do something about those names?" Lilith asks out of the blue...

"What are you talking about, Lady Lilith? Mokemoke's a cute name."

"...? What's Alice got to do with the names of monsters?"

Alice clarifies for me:

"I already explained, didn't I? I'm translating the local language and sending the feed directly to your brain. It's easy for creatures like orcs and griffins, where there's already a word for something similar from Earth, but for completely new and unknown creatures, I've been the one naming them."

"In that case, I agree with Lady Lilith! At least put more effort into the task."

"Could you two leave the bickering for later? They're here!"

As Lilith issues her warning, monsters herded by the Bashin tribe descend on the construction site.

Lilith's tentacles pause their work and turn on the creatures.

"It's been bugging me for a while, but just where do those tentacles of yours sprout from? It's really bothering me, so do you mind if I strip you down to find the answer?"

"Of course I mind! You don't have to help; just don't get in my way."

Lilith politely takes the time to answer me, then, with her lab coat still open, leans forward and widens her eyes.

Looks like she's using her eyes to lock onto targets while putting all her concentration into operating her appendages.

The tentacles start spitting out everything from lightning to lasers to ultrasonic pulses to bullets.

"Man, Lady Lilith's just like a box of chocolates. You never know what you'll get out of her."

"I agree, but shut up. It'll be a hassle if she hears you."

"I can already hear you two! You're in the way just standing there, so go somewhere else for a bit!" Lilith yells at us, her eyes bloodshot, likely from the strain of running her brain at full tilt.

As we back off like we're told, a battle against the monsters unfolds before our eyes.

"Mwa-ha-ha-ha-ha-ha-ha! See, you two? Kisaragi's technology is the greatest! These monsters and savages are out of options and fleeing!"

She's an antisocial character, having hurtled way past the line between madness and genius. She's obsessed with anime and prone to sending people on the stupidest errands imaginable, but she's still a Supreme Leader.

Lilith lets out a satisfied-sounding cackle, single-handedly overwhelming the beasts and tribesmen that gave us such trouble.

What makes her so dangerous is that she doesn't have to worry about running out of ammo or energy.

A chip implanted inside her continually feeds her location to Kisaragi HQ, which then automatically sends energy and ammunition as quickly as she expends them.

I'm told the large-scale teleporter used to send us to this planet is actually based on the technology employed to resupply Lilith's weapons.

"Hmm? Looks like they're going to try a counterattack."

As Lilith scythes through the ranks of their monsters, the Bashin brandish their hand axes and step forward.

There are over twenty of them.

They all draw back and begin hurling their weapons at Lilith.

Most are shot out of the air, and the handful that make it through are effortlessly swatted aside by two tentacles wriggling around Lilith.

Watching this display reminds me of the time I saw Lilith stroll through a battlefield fraught with gunfire as casually as if she were taking a walk.

"...The rules really don't apply to her, do they?" I can't help but mutter, prompting exasperated agreement from Alice.

"What with the tentacles and her title of *Lilith the Black*, Lady Lilith seems a lot better suited to being the Demon Lord."

The scary thing is that Lilith isn't actually putting in much effort yet.

Finding that their throwing axes aren't working, the Bashin begin their retreat.

As though sensing the change, the pretty girls who did a number on our construction equipment emerge from between the trees.

Behind them, I catch a glimpse of the mass of masked and basket-shouldering Hiiragi tribe members.

Seems like the whole gang of guardians are here.

"Lady Lilith, those ones back there are the most dangerous! If the Hiiragi tribe starts dancing, watch out! Also, the girls sprouting from the ground will launch projectiles this way."

I shout my warning to Lilith from a good distance away.

"And? I'm Lilith the Black. Those Hiiragi tribesmen attack using sunlight, yes? In that case…eat this!"

Lilith curls her lips in a confident smirk before fading from view.

It appears she plans to make extensive use of pricey optical-camo technology to neutralize the enemy's light-based weapons.

"Man, Alice, I really want some of that optical camo. I bet I could earn tons of Evil Points if I had that."

"Let me guess, you plan to peep, peep, and peep around some more. Word of warning, you can't use that near a bath. High humidity condenses on the surface, cutting the camo's effectiveness in half."

Dammit, really? And to think that was near the top of my equipment wish list.

The Hiiragi look around in confusion as Lilith disappears before their very eyes. Then they scatter as attacks fire at them from thin air.

That done, Lilith peppers the forest girls with bullets, and they retreat, screeching.

"See, Six? This is the might of Lilith the Black! FYI, I haven't even shown ten percent of my true power!"

"Yeah, yeah, it's quite impressive of you to overwhelm them while still holding back, Lady Lilith. But you know, characters who handicap themselves like that usually end up dying when they have to go all out."

"J-just kidding, Six! That actually took about half my power! You're right, of course. I should use a hundred percent of my power from here on. It's not a good idea to underestimate your opponents."

Perhaps because she's an anime otaku, she seems more than familiar with countless examples of the scenario I've cited, and Lilith quickly walks back her statement.

Turning her back to the Cursed Forest, she resumes her construction efforts where she left off.

"But, Six, you've still got a ways to go, hmm? You're a future Supreme Leader candidate; we can't have you struggling against opposition this pitiful... Still, you were right to call on me out of the three Supreme Leaders for help."

She then happily sticks both her hands into her lab-coat pockets.

"That being the case, Six, you need to show your commitment to becoming a Supreme Leader by engaging in acts of heinous villainy as a Combat Agent for our evil organization. Although, if I'm being honest, I don't hate your softness. You don't have to rush it. I'll wait however long you need."

She gives me a teasing smile.

From deep in the woods, a single beam of light streaks out, blowing away the hideout (still under construction) and sending the posing Lilith tumbling to the ground.

6

The next morning.

"Yo, Alice. Is our useless boss still sleeping?"

"Seems she's awake, but she won't leave her tent. Can't blame her, showing off like that and then, well... Figures she's shutting herself away and staying inside all day."

The sudden detonation of the base did send Lilith tumbling, but since her tentacles intervened at the last minute, she's not actually hurt.

Well, at least, her body's unharmed. That pratfall in the middle of her little spiel left a nasty mark on her pride.

I pick up the breakfast Russell prepared and head to her tent.

"Lady Lilith, how long do you plan to pout? It's fine. It's common knowledge among the Kisaragi rank and file that you're kind of useless. It's nothing we didn't already know."

"...?!"

I hear a sharp inhalation as the tent's occupant swallows a comeback. I guess she was clueless about her reputation in the organization.

There's a rustling as something crawls around inside the tent, then Lilith's face peeks out.

"...That reminds me, Six. I didn't think much of it at first, but where are Tiger Man and the other agents?"

Her composure restored, it finally occurs to Lilith to ask about the rest of our troops.

"After hearing you would be the one reinforcing us, Lady Lilith, they scattered to the four winds."

"Wh-why?! Um...wait, does everyone hate me?!"

Despite the fact that she seems the type least likely to care about things like that among the Supreme Leaders, Lilith chooses this moment to get self-conscious.

"......"

"Six, now isn't the time for you to get all quiet. You're supposed to reassure me! Tell me that's not the case! Wh-what am I doing wrong? I'll do my best to fix it, so tell me what I'm doing wrong!"

I mean, she wouldn't be so bad if it weren't for the fact that she uses us like errand boys. That and the whole batshit-crazy thing...

"Well, there's a pretty long list, but... First, Lady Lilith, compared with Lady Astaroth and Lady Belial, you're completely lacking in the sex-appeal department."

"Any last words?"

Lilith, beautiful but modest where it counts, mutters darkly.

"I'm only telling you what you wanted to know, but if that's how it's gonna be, whatever. Don't blame me when the agents you send to bring you food put weird stuff in it."

"I'm sorry! I'll try to fix things, honest! So please… But there isn't a whole lot I can do about sex appeal, y'know!"

Lilith crawls out of the tent with tears in her eyes, pleading as she clings to my leg.

"Your problem, Lady Lilith, is you eat nothing but junk food. Considering that, it's probably too late to try to address your lack of assets, so why not start by revealing a bit more?"

"I really don't need you telling me it's probably too late! I'm a scientist. If there's even a one percent chance, I'll keep fighting, even if it's against fate itself."

She's trying to make it sound impressive, but given the context, ehh…

"But…more revealing…? Wouldn't showing more skin just make me look kind of stupid?"

"When it comes to reputation, you're already at rock bottom, Lady Lilith. You're so far down, it's all up from here. Lose the tacky lab coat. Wearing it doesn't make you seem any smarter."

"Can't you, I don't know, be a little more tactful?! All right, fine, I'll try making my outfits more revealing. But surely, there are other reasons, right? If agents are avoiding me just because I'm not showing enough skin, I'm going to have to beat some sense into them."

Other reasons? Hmm, I guess all that's left is…

"Well, beyond that, you just need to stop sending us on stupid errands and using us as subjects for your crazy experiments…"

"Wait, isn't that the bigger issue?! The bit about how I dress is kind of irrelevant, isn't it?! Forget all this for now. Let's get our base built today!"

Slightly motivated by our exchange, Lilith grabs her breakfast and scarfs it down.

*   *   *

Back at the construction site.

The location has grown familiar by now, but we got some news today. We've figured out who's behind the explosions.

According to Alice, what sniped our hideout yesterday is some new form of monster.

One moment, there was a flash of light from deep in the woods, and the next, *boom* went the base, with Lilith sent flying.

A look at the light source revealed a large reptile poking its head out of the ground.

Basically, we'd successfully executed Alice's plan: Build a decoy to draw out the bomber.

"...All right, then. Ready, Six, Alice? The enemy is a large monster that takes cover underground between long-range attacks. Now that we know what it is, we can take care of it!"

Lilith's specialty is long-range shelling using a massive amount of modern artillery.

Her typical MO is to use overwhelming firepower to vaporize a wide area, turning it into a charred wasteland. However...

"While we have no problem with you strafing the woods, please don't use any of your really dangerous stuff."

"I mean, the really dangerous stuff is the most efficient way of reducing things to rubble, but that wouldn't be elegant. However, I, in my peerless genius, have already planned for this! Last night, while you lot were snoring away, I launched a small surveillance satellite into orbit. I've already identified the target's lair."

In spite of everything, she's still a Supreme Leader. She's planned ahead.

I turn to Lilith as she starts scribbling a note. I guess she intends to request some equipment.

"Why can't you put all that strategizing to better use anyway?"

"Shut up, Six. You simpletons just can't understand how a genius like myself operates. Now, while we don't know what method the enemy uses to attack, we can always figure that out after we kill it. And with that… 'Hypersonic Anti-Submarine Depth Charge!'"

As Lilith happily holds up the compact depth charge, I sigh in exasperation.

"Lady Lilith, you know that'll mess up the bedrock around here. We're supposed to settle this area, remember? We haven't even done a tectonic survey yet. What if you cause an earthquake?"

"So what? If there's the possibility of an earthquake, we might as well find out about it *before* we start moving people here. It keeps the damage to a minimum. That's the power of science!"

The Hypersonic Anti-Submarine Depth Charge.

It's a weapon particularly hated by people like the Japanese, who've been plagued by earthquakes throughout history. The hatred is justified, though. It's been used to artificially trigger earthquakes more than once.

Lilith stole…or rather, got the inspiration from…the popular monster-hunting game, *Monster Panda*, where one uses sonic explosives to force subterranean enemies to the surface.

The weapon is primarily intended to be deployed against underground bases, but it's also been used countless times to trigger earthquakes in areas where a large quake was anticipated within a matter of decades. Of course, in addition to the quakes, it also triggered massive protests from multiple activist groups.

Groups that believe it's best to evacuate the areas and get the quakes over with. Groups that believe that, if left alone, the quakes might never happen and that consider it hubris to try to control nature. Groups that believe even broaching the subject completely discounts the feelings of the victims. These factions have been locked in a never-ending debate since we triggered the first quake.

Just then, Alice breaks her silence.

"Preach, Lady Lilith. There is nothing science can't do. Someday, humanity will overcome any disaster. You might be useless from time to time, but you make good points!"

"Of course. Victory to humanity as we close the books on our long history of fighting natural disasters... Hey, Alice, are you sure you don't need maintenance? I'm your creator, you know..."

As the science cultists work themselves up into a lather, the forest begins stirring, as though sensing the danger.

The trees suddenly part, and from the new opening, a giant lizard shows its face...

"Looks like it detected the danger through natural instinct. But it's too late! Depth charge, awaaaay!"

Lilith's tentacle grabs the explosive and tosses it at the lizard's head.

The distance is about two kilometers.

Despite the considerable range, the anti-submarine depth charge sails high into the sky, falling in a pinpoint arc toward the target and—

A sharp, keening noise pierces the air as the ground violently rumbles underfoot.

The quake passes in a few seconds. Struck by the hypersonic blast from the depth charge, the lizard leaps out of the ground and rolls around in pain.

"Damn, Alice, she really did just cause an earthquake."

"Impressive, Lady Lilith. Supreme Leaders are something else."

"Hold on. That wasn't an earthquake. It was over too quickly! And I didn't get the Evil Points Acquired announcement! A-anyway, we've managed to drag the target aboveground!"

Panicking a little, Lilith turns her tentacles toward the lizard still thrashing around in the dirt.

7

With the giant lizard dead, the rest of the monsters withdraw like a receding tide.

I guess the lizard must have been the pack leader around here.

The science nerds insist on checking out the corpse, so we're about to head toward the target when…

"Wait, whaaat?!"

Lilith lets out a cry of surprise as she glances down at her device.

"What is it, Lady Lilith? Was that earthquake actually your fault, Lady Lilith? Did you get a massive influx of Evil Points?"

"No! I already told you I didn't get the point announcement! But when I double-checked my score, my point total was a lot lower than it should be…"

Alice helpfully elaborates as Lilith keeps rechecking her device in shock.

"While you're on this planet, all supplies are going to cost you Evil Points. Basically, after your battle, Lady Lilith, the points were spent on your automatic resupply of ammunition and energy cartridges for your energy weapons. You were generous with your ammo yesterday, after all."

"Wait just a minute. That applies to leaders like me, too?!"

On Earth, the cost of ammunition and energy cartridges that Lilith uses is automatically deducted from her bank account.

But on this planet, even things that are cheap to buy with cash require payment in Evil Points.

This clause was originally put in place to force me to commit acts of villainy whether I liked it or not, but…

"Are you kidding me?! My strength is based on the fact that I have access to unlimited ammo! If I stay here, I won't be useful for long!"

Flipping out when a policy of her own making comes back to bite her—what a lovely boss.

"No one's kidding. That's your own damn rule, remember! You might spend your days goofing off, but since you're here, we need you to do actual work. If you spend all your Evil Points and still end up useless, I'm gonna take out my pent-up frustration on you! You're going to understand at least SOME of my suffering!"

"Noooooooooo! I don't wannnnnnnaaaaaaaaaa!"

As Lilith tries to return to the camp, we spend the next hour cajoling her with a mixture of threats and reassurances.

Finally getting out of her funk, our bothersome leader makes her way to the target.

"Wow, that's big. Dinosaur-class, even. How is it supporting its own body...?"

Lilith speaks with a hint of surprise, looking up at the giant lizard sprawled out with a huge hole through its head.

It really is a giant lizard, and it's big enough that if someone told you it was actually a dinosaur, you'd likely believe them.

"Damn, giant lizards are sick. Hey, Alice, let's try eating this thing. Then when I get back to Earth, I'm gonna brag about eating dinosaur steak."

"Just because you Combat Agents are tough doesn't mean you should go around putting random things in your mouth... Huh."

After patting the lizard's body with her hands, Alice quizzically tilts her head.

"What, you want a slice of dino-steak, too?"

"I don't eat, you idiot. But try touching it. The skin feels metallic."

I reach over and touch the lizard, and just as she says, the skin feels solid and cool to the touch.

With her interest piqued, Lilith begins taking a skin sample. I wander over and open the beast's jaws.

""Oh...""

Alice and I peer inside the mouth.

"What is it? …Oh-ho-ho, well, well…"

Lilith joins us in staring into the creature's maw.

The lizard's innards are mechanical.

There appears to be a deployable turret inside its mouth. I have to guess that's what blew away our hideout.

It's then that I notice the hole in the ground the lizard popped its head out of also looks faintly metallic.

"Lady Lilith, Lady Lilith, notice anything odd about this thing's lair?"

"…Any way you look at it, it's clearly a highly advanced, man-made structure," says Lilith curiously, directing her tentacles toward the ground.

Is she searching underground with sonar or something?

"…Hah! Ah-ha-ha-ha-ha-ha! Six, Alice, listen up! There's a giant subterranean facility in this region! This is getting really interesting! Tell the other agents to be careful when exploring this place! Any damage will be met with severe punishment!"

As Lilith cackles maniacally, Alice and I peer into the giant hole.

"…Um, the facilities are a wreck thanks to the depth charge you used, Lady Lilith."

"…Okay, tell the others to…uh…just be careful when they're down there…"

CHAPTER 2

🐾 Vs. the Sky King

1

Following the discovery of the mysterious facility, we managed to strong-arm Lilith into putting aside her tantrums about spending more points, forcing her to wipe out the worst of the monsters nearby before returning to our campsite. The day after...

Currently, the other agents are off using heavy equipment Lilith provided in a display of generosity, working under Alice's direction to resume construction.

As for me...

"How's this, Six? I switched to a short-sleeved lab coat, so I'm showing off a little more skin now. What do you think?"

"I think that, despite all your smarts, you're actually kind of dumb, Lady Lilith."

I'm stuck at our campsite babysitting Lilith, since everyone else foisted the responsibility on me.

"What?! I take your advice, and your reaction is to make fun of me?!"

"When I said show more skin, I meant show off your midriff or lower your neckline or something. All you did was switch to a summer lab coat."

Having completely misconstrued what I told her, Lilith had rolled up her sleeves, showing off her upper arms here and there.

Me, I've taken off my typical power armor and put on a formal black suit.

Today, at Lilith's request, we're meeting with this country's de facto ruler, Tillis.

Currently, the relationship between Tillis's domain and Kisaragi is in a delicate balance.

From the leadership's point of view, they want to use diplomacy to bring this kingdom into the fold without bloodshed.

"So, Lady Lilith, what's the plan for taking over this country?"

I'm pretty sure that Alice, who's a lot cleverer than her creator, has already tried a few different negotiating tactics.

"Why, we'll go with gunboat diplomacy, of course. This nation owes us a bit already for the agents we deployed, starting with you, Six. We can come up with some pretexts related to that and make some unreasonable demands! If they won't capitulate, we'll threaten to force them under our banner!"

"Whoo! That's mighty evil of you, Lady Lilith! That's exactly what I expect from the winner of the Most Antisocial Leader and Most Scheming Leader surveys!"

"Heh, now, now, flattery won't get you much more than spending money, Six... Say, who conducts those extra surveys? If you just tell me, I won't get mad or anything..."

Grace Kingdom, Princess Tillis's chambers.

"Welcome, welcome! I've been looking forward to discussing matters with a member of the Kisaragi leadership!"

"You have our apologies! Our sincerest, deepest apologies! But our agents need to conduct acts of villainy in order to protect your kingdom…"

After hearing about what we were doing on our way to the castle, Lilith bobs her head up and down in apologetic bows.

"Indeed! Evil Points, was it? We're well aware of that necessity. Which is why there are standing orders to ignore little acts of misbehavior on the part of your agents."

"And we sincerely appreciate your—"

"However!"

The wily scientist, pride of the Kisaragi Corporation, is at a disadvantage against the scheming princess.

Which is to be expected. The kingdom just has way too much ammo to use against us.

"However, the moment we think to thank them for fixing our kingdom's artifact, they implement a terrifyingly unacceptable activation prayer! No sooner do we send them to escort our diplomat to another country than they go ahead and trigger a war!"

"Y-y-you have our sincerest apologies!"

This is hopeless. Alice is a much better negotiator.

"Just recently, your employees began sneaking into my bedroom, and while I slept, they played Jenga, had a cookout, and, to top it off, attempted to go to the bathroom! Why would anyone think to relieve themselves, *naked*, inside a maiden's bedroom?! None of this makes any sense! Please explain their logic to me!"

"I'm sorry, I'm sorry, I'm sorry, I'm sorry! I honestly don't understand it, either!"

There isn't even a hint of the confidence she was showing earlier, and she's currently getting trounced.

I try to subtly offer my struggling boss a bit of help.

"Lady Lilith, Lady Lilith. You need to put more emphasis on my exploits. I've taken out some of the competition's leadership, for example."

"Oh, right. You need to take the exploits of our Agent Six into consideration! I believe it's quite the achievement to have taken out some of the leaders of the so-called Demon Lord's Army!"

At my whisper, Lilith suddenly returns to the offensive...

"On the matter of eliminating the leaders of the Demon Lord's Army, we've already paid out a substantial reward to Miss Alice..."

"Oh?"

...only to be promptly batted aside.

Oh, that's right. I remember Alice telling me something about getting a huge bonus.

She said I'd spend it all if I got the whole amount, so she's been doling it out daily as an allowance.

"Indeed, our kingdom is paying a monthly stipend as a defense fee to all your agents, Sir Six included. The amount is greater than what we pay our own knights!"

"Oh! That's right! Lady Lilith, the pay that we're getting from the kingdom's actually more than our pay from Kisaragi! Considering how long I've been working for Kisaragi, that's messed up, isn't it?!"

Lilith twitches hearing this.

She's reminded that in my reports I noted I was getting paid more by this kingdom than by Kisaragi.

"...Yes, now that I've mentioned it...Sir Six, why not bring the other agents with you and become knights of our kingdom...?"

"Well...! Today was only intended to serve as an introduction! Six, we've taken enough of Her Highness's time, don't you think? We hope you'll continue using Kisaragi's services in the future!"

As Lilith attempts to leave the room with that remark, I hold her in place.

"When I last made this request of Miss Alice, she rejected it out of hand, but I would like to ask once again! Please provide us with technology! Share your advancements with our kingdom!"

"I request an improvement to my employment conditions! Give me a raise! Give me time-off! Or I'll switch sides, dammit!"

"All right, all right! Both of you, calm down!"

2

On the way home from the castle.

"Well, now you've done it, Six. I've got a whole lot more headaches to deal with. I mean, what sort of life do you have to live to even come up with the idea of pooping in a princess's room?"

"Don't pin all the blame on me. Ten's the one who tried to poop in Tillis's room."

After accepting Tillis's request to transfer technology, Lilith's been muttering complaints next to me.

"Why are my subordinates all such a handful?"

"They probably take after their boss."

While Lilith and I are bantering—

"This one's too lame to bring any glory! Surely, you have better targets! Something like a spy who's infiltrated the city or an infamous criminal everyone's heard of!!"

—I hear a familiar voice and turn toward it, catching sight of Snow arguing with a shady character.

"You say that, Miss Snow, but my information's primarily about monsters. Whenever I get a tip about a criminal, I just turn around and sell it to the guards."

The shady-looking man must be an information broker or something.

"I get that, but that's why I'm asking for your help! With your nose for knowledge, I'm sure you're aware I've been hit with a pay cut. I'm broke! We've known each other a long time! Do me a favor and give me a tip about a criminal with a bounty on his head!"

"Look, I can't just pull someone like that out of my... Oh, wait, I do have someone in mind. An infamous criminal everyone's heard of."

At the broker's words, Snow's face lights up.

"Please! Who is it? Where is he?!"

"The criminal's name is the Fly. And he's standing right behind you."

At that, Snow turns around, sees me, and pounces.

"Six, who is this girl who suddenly attacked you? You two seem acquainted, but I suggest you pick your friends better."

"She's one of my subordinates. Her name is Snow."

"Mmmph! Mrrrrrm!"

Snow lies at my feet, constricted head to toe by one of Lilith's tentacles.

As I'm driving off the information broker who ratted me out as a criminal, Lilith studies Snow rather closely.

"...Ah, I see. So this is the girl who figured out you were a spy. I've read all about you in the reports. Welcome to the Kisaragi Corporation! We're happy to invite talented people into our ranks! I'm one of the Supreme Leaders of the Kisaragi Corporation, Lilith the Black!"

"Mrrmph?! Mmff, mmfffmmph!"

Snow appears to have something to say. I just assume it's something along the lines of *I'm a knight of this realm; I have no intention of joining Kisaragi!*

"Lady Lilith, she may be my subordinate, but she's got nothing to do with Kisaragi. She's still with this kingdom, but she's been assigned by Tillis to help me out. Plus, she's always pissed at me for one reason or another."

Hearing this, Lilith gazes into Snow's stubborn expression and smiles happily.

"Ah, I see. I can sense that she's got a strong will for resisting evil influence. The pleasure and points derived from luring a righteous person like her to evil is unparalleled!"

"Mrrrrmmmph! Frrrrmph!"

Snow glares defiantly, her angry retorts muffled by the tentacles.

"Bwa-ha-ha-ha, good! A wonderful find! Do resist as best as you can. When you're prepared to serve us, gently close your eyes and nod! …Let's see, we should start with her family. Six, go look up her family roster. These sorts are usually pretty quick to fall when their loved ones are held for ransom."

"If I recall, she's actually an orphan from the slums. I don't think she has any family."

"Mmph!"

At Snow's and my reactions, Lilith stops cackling.

"So family members are out… Okay, next! The reports said you're a knight. A knight's duty is to protect people. Then let's see that in action… Which means, Six, you're going to help me out with this one."

"W-wait, what are you doing, Lady Lilith? This isn't funny!"

After wrapping me up in tentacles like Snow, Lilith holds a heavy rock in front of me.

"Listen up. I'm going to suspend this rock from a length of rope. Under the rock will be Six's head. And you, Miss Snow, will be holding the rope back with your teeth."

What the hell?!

"Wait, think about this, Lady Lilith! Think about how badly that'd mess up my head!"

"Your head's already messed up, so that's not a concern. Never mind that, Six, and pay attention. People like her are always going on about protecting the weak, but let's see just how hypocritical the truly weak can be when push comes to shove! There's nothing I love more than revealing their true colors!"

Yeah, Lilith's a piece of work, all right.

She giddily sets about readying the scenario, but I admit I'm kind of interested to see how this will play out.

Come to think of it, the constricted woman tasked with saving me *has* kissed me before.

She's basically a textbook *tsundere*.

Maybe she'll actually fight pretty hard for me. Could it be that, deep down, she really has a thing for me?

With her preparations finished, Lilith flashes a smile worthy of a mad scientist and makes a declaration to Snow.

"Six's head is now in your hands. A precious comrade. A beloved friend. Your dearest lover. When someone like that is placed on a scale with your life on the other end, which will you choose?"

The rock dangles over my head, a tentacle holding the other end of the rope.

Lilith removes the tentacle covering Snow's mouth and extends the rope to her.

"One more thing. If you can hold on for one full minute—"

Before Lilith can finish, Snow grabs the rope with her mouth, arches her back as she pulls it taut, then lets it go without a moment's hesitation.

"Yeowwwwwww!"

"H-hey, wh-what do you think you're doing?! Six! That sounded pretty bad. Are you all right?"

Having had a largish rock dropped on my skull, I protest by writhing back and forth.

"Of course I'm not all right! You should've known this would happen! Let go of me, Lady Lilith! I'm gonna treat this defenseless cocoon bitch to some real punishment!"

With a giant bump growing on my head, I start kicking Snow, totally ignoring the tentacles wrapped around me.

"Honorable Knights of Grace don't submit to evil!"

"Oh, shut up! As if you're ever remotely knightlike in your

day-to-day life! Hell, I saw you pull that rope back! You did that on purpose to make it hurt more, didn't you?!"

"So what if I did, you criminal?! I realized my life's been going downhill ever since I met you. Kisaragi?! Evil organization?! Screw that! I'm done with you all! Just leave me alone!"

Snow returns the kicks, firing off a list of complaints while still tied up by tentacles.

"What's with this girl…? If using family members or trying to break her commitment to justice won't work, the only thing left is to bribe her with money or material wealth…"

The moment those words pass Lilith's lips, Snow freezes in place.

"…I'm not even going to demand you leave the kingdom's service. Why don't we start you off with a trial period as a Combat Agent? You can get paid by both Grace and our organization, like Six."

"Hmph…! Do you really expect the former knight captain of the Royal Guard to be lured by such sweet words, Lady Lilith? What else?! What other benefits does Kisaragi offer?!"

As the hog-tied knight begins adopting a more respectful tone, Lilith continues, albeit a little incredulously.

"Kisaragi's salary might be low, but we offer great benefits. We have workplace injury compensation and a pension plan, so if you lose the ability to work after getting hurt, we'll provide everything you need to live out the rest of your life in peace. Also…if I recall, you're fond of blades and swords, right? Our organization has a collection of master-crafted swords that don't exist on this—"

Before Lilith finishes, Snow gently closes her eyes.

3

Guided by the newly released Snow, we've arrived at a certain facility.

"This is the water-treatment plant. It's practically unused these days. What are you planning to do?"

Water in this kingdom is precious.

We've got Russell making water right now, but if something happens to him, the current system will collapse.

The water-treatment facility surrounds a large well, but after a quick look, anyone can see it's dry.

"We're going to use Kisaragi technology to revive this well. The water likely dried up because they exhausted the shallow aquifer. Digging deeper should bring up more water."

Seems Lilith plans to fulfill her promise to Tillis from earlier.

I whisper to her as she peers down the well.

"*Lady Lilith, Lady Lilith, are you sure we should be sharing technology without checking with headquarters?*"

"*We're going to give them harmless tech before they start asking for things like weapons. Besides, deep well drilling isn't particularly advanced from our point of view. It's a good way to show the locals our superiority. To the ignorant, sufficiently advanced technology is indistinguishable from magic. Let's have these Neanderthals worship us like gods.*"

Wow, as expected of a Supreme Leader of an evil organization; she naturally looks down on the locals.

"*That's pretty scummy, but I wanna be worshipped, too. Can I be in your entourage?*"

"*Sure, so long as you stay out of my way. You can be in charge of lighting my cigars.*"

"*But, Lady Lilith, you don't smoke.*"

Snow tilts her head quizzically at our hushed conversation.

"I appreciate your offer to revive that well, but you should probably do it elsewhere. I heard that when they tried to dig deeper here, they got water contaminated with a black, gooey substance."

"Miss Snow, was it? Come and tell me more about it."

"Lady Lilith, I wanna buy a luxury condo full of hot women and drink champagne every day."

Snow seems a bit put off by our sudden change in attitude.

"What good will that do you? I'll note ahead of time that any resources that come out of the ground belong to the kingdom and need permission from higher up…"

"Miss Snow. This black water is completely useless to you but very valuable to us. It will take many decades of technological development for you to benefit from it, but if you sell it to us, we can have a mutually profitable, win-win relationship…"

As Lilith begins trying to seriously convince Snow, I interject:

"Lady Lilith, Lady Lilith, when dealing with this one, you need to make things easier to understand… Hey, Snow, if you forget about this black water, we'll give you a cut of the profits. Also…what sort of katana would you like?"

"I have no idea what black water you're talking about, but I'd like a sword that's a bit longer than the one I got from Sir Tiger Man the other day. Also, if you're going to dig here, let me go get permission from above right now. You can get started right away."

Lilith watches as Snow's attitude does a complete one-eighty and the knight dashes off, before mentioning as an aside:

"You know, Six, you need to choose your subordinates more carefully."

"Pretty sure she's the best fit for Kisaragi out of all my troops."

She's particularly obsessed with money and glory, but she's also the easiest to understand.

After recovering, Lilith smiles confidently.

"Well, either way, we have permission to begin digging. If it's gushing out at this depth, you can bet there's a big oil reserve under this land! Mwa-ha-ha-ha! We're rich, Six—rich!"

"Impressive, Lady Lilith! The fact that you have no intention of reporting any of this to HQ is awesome!"

"I know, I know! Praise me more!"

I don't know how she plans to refine the oil she'll dig up, but she's one of the Supreme Leaders. I'm sure she's got a black-market connection or two.

Lilith happily scribbles out an order and begins assembling the teleported drilling equipment with her tentacles.

"All right, let's do a test drill! Depending on the quality and volume of the oil reserves, we might have to build a giant oil refinery here! Mwa-ha-ha-ha-ha-ha! The future's looking bright, Six! ...Oh, that's funny."

As Lilith hits peak enthusiasm and begins digging, a black, gooey liquid seeps out of the ground, filling the bottom of the well.

But it doesn't look very oil-like.

I spent a lot of time at an oil refinery while on a mission in the Middle East, so I can tell something's up.

"Lady Lilith, is this really oil?"

"Th-that's strange. It looks odd to me, too..."

There's definitely something off here.

It just looks like liquid, but my sense of danger, acquired through years of experience, is telling me to proceed with caution...

Suddenly, the black goo attacks Lilith.

"Whaaaaaaaa—?! W-wait, what is this?! Six! SIIIX!"

"Lady Lilith, it's a slime! It's the perverted kind that melts the clothing of pretty girls and leaves them naked!"

Fending off the slime with her tentacles, Lilith looks to me in a teary-eyed panic.

"This is bad, Six! I'm going to end up like a porn-game character! Request weapons that work on slimes!"

The slime's getting to be a decent size as it continues flowing out of the well.

It's gonna be tricky for her to block the whole thing, even with all her tentacles.

"I'm sorry, Lady Lilith, but this is a pretty rare opportunity. Can I watch a little longer?"

"You can keep watching if you're prepared to face my wrath once I've dealt with this slime!"

Feeling an imminent threat to my well-being, I decide to do as she says.

…Um, wait.

"Uh, Lady Lilith, this is a problem. I'm not allowed to spend Evil Points right now!"

"Gaaaaaah! That's right! Six, take my memo pad from my lab coat! You can use my teleporter and points! I'm too busy controlling my tentacles right now!"

As Lilith shouts, her expression fixed in extreme concentration, I reach for her lab coat…

"You're not gonna accuse me of sexual harassment or anything later, right? There's nothing funny about getting called out for harassment later just for helping you."

"I won't! And it's in the side pocket. Just where the hell were you planning to dig?!"

I grab the memo pad and teleporter from her pocket and order a weapon that would work against a slime…

"What even works against slimes? Is it like a slug? Maybe a salt bomb?"

"How the hell should I know?! Get something like a flamethrower or some liquid nitrogen!"

A flamethrower and liquid nitrogen—got it.

"Lady Lilith, I'd like new volumes of some manga I've fallen behind on. Can I order them, too?"

"Do whatever you want! But, Six, you better remember you're paying for it later!"

That's unfortunate. I'm so good at forgetting things that even Alice is impressed by it.

Lilith tearily fights off the slime as I hum a little tune and scribble out my memo. Just then—

"Wh-what the hell are you two doing?!"

Snow, who went out to get permission from her higher-ups, runs down the stairs, drawing her magic sword.

Attacking with her burning blade, Snow drives the slime, which evidently dislikes heat, back into the well.

"Six, order some quick-drying concrete from headquarters! We're sealing this damned well!"

Lilith gasps out the order between ragged breaths as I quickly scribble with my pen.

"W-wait, but what about my share? And my katana?"

"That black water isn't the stuff we were looking for, so…"

I do add a single katana to the list and send it to headquarters.

A moment later, a pile of quick-drying concrete arrives, along with a shovel, new manga, and a sword—

"Here, have the katana."

"Whoo-hoo!"

"Okay, Six, come over here!"

After burying the first well in cement, we travel to another at Snow's direction.

"You know, you could've mentioned it was a slime instead of giving us vague warnings about black water."

"How was I supposed to know? They only told me they stopped drilling wells because of the black water," responds Snow, smirking as she looks over the blade acquired with Lilith's Evil Points.

And then…

"Could you please get over it already, Lady Lilith? It's just a little prank from your adorable subordinate."

"Grrr...this son of a— I want to just punch him... Forget it, we're not digging any more wells. What if that thing comes up again?"

Lilith sulks.

"Mm...well, can't blame you after that encounter. And I've heard digging wells isn't a job for amateurs. But the fact that you were willing to help our kingdom is worth..."

As Snow smiles, trying to reassure Lilith, I thrust out my hand to cut her off.

"Don't be ridiculous! Nothing's impossible for our Lady Lilith! She can dig a well in no time! We're going to show you just what Lady Lilith's capable of! Go gather a crowd!"

"H-hold on!"

As I snap a retort that Lilith would undoubtedly have wanted me to say, a group of onlookers begins gathering, a consequence of this particular well being near the center of town.

"Lady Lilith, we've got quite a crowd here. This is a good chance to show them your abilities!"

"Ah, dammit! Well, I do suppose water is the most important resource for humanity. Very well, just watch as I begin the process of converting the wastelands and deserts outside the city into fertile plains! Science is superior to nature!"

Lilith had once tried turning land we'd conquered in the Sahara Desert into a green woodland.

She'd started talking about using natto bacteria to retain water, leading to a massive protest by the local residents.

Can't blame them. No one wants natto scattered around the desert.

I'd protest for sure.

"Turning things green is great and all, but could you not leave natto all over the place this time? That was messed up, even for us."

"I never told you to throw natto around! I told you Combat Agents to convert it into water-retaining natto resin before distributing it! How many times did I have to say it...?!"

As Lilith spouts nonsense, Snow ignores her and directs a speech at the onlookers.

"Starting in a moment, these people I have brought will return water to this well! Once the well is revived, be sure to tell everyone..."

Seems she's trying to use this opportunity to garner some glory for herself.

"Hey, Six, you really need to choose your subordinates more carefully."

"Just as we can't pick our ideal bosses, subordinates can also be hit-or-miss."

4

Three hours after we start drilling the well.

"Lady Lilith, there's no water coming out, the crowd left, and I'm getting bored."

"This is really odd, given that we're using a super-high-tech Kisaragi drill. Well, in theory, if we keep digging and digging, something'll come out eventually. Let's just leave it running on autopilot."

It's an incredibly expensive piece of equipment that no Combat Agent would have the Evil Points to requisition, but a Supreme Leader like Lilith can just leave it running.

As I'm watching the drilling, Snow comes by and asks:

"Hey, Six, are you sure this'll actually produce water? If so, I'm thinking of borrowing some money and buying up the land around here."

Water in this kingdom is precious.

If the well starts producing again, the surrounding land is going to shoot up in value.

That's definitely true, but...

"Far be it from me to mention, but lately, there's been no trace of chivalry to your actions. What happened to the proud knight I first met?"

"Quiet, Six. Knights have to eat and put clothes on their backs. I need money to survive. I don't want to hear it from someone who's getting an allowance from Alice."

Lilith watches our exchange and chuckles.

"You know, despite it all, you two seem pretty close. Heh-heh, Six, shouldn't you be more careful? If Astaroth sees you like this..."

She snickers teasingly.

"Can you knock it off, Lady Lilith? We're really not like that. Not with this one."

"On this, we agree. I'd prefer someone with money."

"I—I see... Sorry about that. I didn't expect you two to so vigorously deny it... Anyway, let's leave the rest to the drill, and—"

I interrupt Lilith before she can finish.

"Hey, Snow, next! C'mon, next! I'm pretty good at solving problems in developing countries. After water, we need to deal with food! With Lilith's brains, we can do a tech transfer to get you all the food you could possibly need! Viva la Lilithification!"

"H-hold on!"

Despite Lilith looking like she wants to say something, we drag her along to our next destination...

"This is our kingdom's farming facility."

The two of us look up at the building.

"Lady Lilith. This just looks like a normal factory to me."

"Yes, Six, this is, indeed, a factory."

It's a modern building that looks completely out of place on a fantasy world.

In stark contrast to its surroundings sits a concrete factory that wouldn't be out of place in Japan.

"What do we do, Lady Lilith? Factory farming? Only a handful of places do that on Earth. I don't think Lilithification is gonna work here."

"W-well, hold on, Six. It's too early to panic. Let's take a look inside and see if they're actually doing hydroponics here."

Lilith suggests this with naked confusion before stepping foot into the factory.

"Huh...? What the hell is this...?" mutters Lilith, in a daze as she peeks inside. I follow her into the building.

"...Lady Lilith, I have to admit I underestimated the bastards of this kingdom. They're more ruthless than I thought."

"Yeah, I thought they were better people until I saw this..."

It's closer to a forced-labor camp than a factory.

Inside, orcs and other humanoid creatures are working farm plots.

Above the plots float mysterious objects, which resemble fireflies and emit a bright light, illuminating the enclosed factory space.

"Snow, get your ass over here."

"Six, it's slavery. Fantasy is scary. Developing countries are super scary. Prisoners have no rights here..."

Snow looks puzzled that we're taken aback.

"What? Your farms don't make use of livestock?"

"Lady Lilith, she just called them livestock."

"Well, sure, we used to employ beasts of burden back in the day for hard labor and stuff...but humanoids? No, nothing like that. We used horses and cows for plowing fields, but this sort of thing is generally frowned upon..."

Japan had a slavery system for farming back in the Warring States period, and given the level of culture and technology here, I suppose slaves and serfs were to be expected, but...

"I don't know what hang-ups you're having, but this is a mutually beneficial and highly efficient system. We capture relatively tame wild orcs who can't survive on their own, protect them, and provide them with food in exchange for working our fields. Once they reach the end of their life spans, we show our appreciation by eating them. Seems like a very rational system if you ask me…"

"This is evil, Six. Pure evil. She just said they exploit their labor and then eat them when they die… They eat humanoids!"

Despite being a Supreme Leader, Lilith's a bit of a lightweight who's now recoiling from Snow.

"Yep, they eat those humanoid monsters. And did you know they can even speak our languages?"

"Pure evil. Six, this is pure, depraved evil!"

We reel from the realization that this kingdom's farming system is so ruthlessly efficient that it puts an evil organization to shame. Snow tilts her head and quips:

"You did the same thing, yes? Aside from the fact that they resemble humans and can speak, what's the difference? Here, in this otherwise dangerous world, they can live lives of relative peace. In exchange, we get labor and meat. It's the whole WIN-WIN situation you two are so fond of."

"Yeah…that's not quite it…"

"They're your farming companions, yet you eat them in the end? I don't get that part. Not one bit."

This must be the difference between civilized people and barbarians.

"Your country must be extremely peaceful and rich in food…"

I mean, the orcs don't exactly look oppressed.

Ethics aside, it's certainly rational…

…Lilith points at one of the lights as if to change the subject.

"What are those floating things? They're too big and too bright to be fireflies. I mean, they're bright enough to raise crops."

Guess her curiosity as a scientist is overriding her other instincts.

"Oh, those are fairies."

""Fairies…""

Hearing Snow's serious tone, we repeat the word in unison.

"Yes, fairies. They're tame creatures that can't survive without clean water, so in this region, where water is scarce, they're having quite the tough time. We have them live inside our factory so that they can shine their lights. This allows us to grow vegetables year-round."

Upon closer inspection, we notice faint humanoid shapes within the intense lights.

These bastards... If they can find a use for them, they'll even exploit adorable creatures.

I'm starting to think Kisaragi's the model of corporate social responsibility.

"...Wait, why are you so fixated on farming indoors? Sure, the sun's a little strong, but you have plenty of land. Wouldn't it be better to farm outside?"

"...? Are the farms of your home world not plagued by flying monsters?"

Oh yeah, this is a fantasy world.

Yeah, if a giant flying monster like a griffin landed on a farm, the crops wouldn't last very long.

"You know, this planet's pretty harsh... There are obviously upsides to conquering it, but..."

"Doing something about that is your job, Lady Lilith. You can Lilithificate things by teaching them how to deal with flying pests."

Although crows are the worst of the airborne scourges in Japan, I constantly catch glimpses of things like wyverns on this planet.

An antipest net won't do much good against those.

"...Wellll, all right. We could try surrounding the farms with giant cages. No, no, that's not much different from the factory-farming system they've got now... Do we exterminate the flying vermin? ...Given that we're already struggling with the monsters in the woods, that's not going to be easy..."

Lilith folds her arms against her chest, muttering to herself in thought.

Still, the only thing I can think of is to put automated antiair gun turrets in the middle of the farm.

Let's leave the thinking to the smart people…

"Pesticides! Pesticides are the answer, Six! Let's scatter some powerful pesticides and grow crops that the monsters can't eat! It's perfect. I've got a fantastic pesticide I developed a long time ago. It was so strong, it'd even kill people. Monsters stand no chance against it!"

"Okay, Lady Lilith, now I'm sure you're just plain crazy."

I mean, all she needs to do is drive away the pests, not kill them.

…Oh, wait!

"I know! Lady Lilith, I have a great idea! Pee! Pee is the key! You're ultra-powerful, Lady Lilith, so give me some of your pee!"

"I'm sorry, what? If you take one more step in my direction, I *will* shoot you."

Seems even with her genius intellect, Lilith can't quite comprehend the pee solution.

"Why are you being so difficult, Lady Lilith…? If you're opposed to it, I'll go ask for Tiger Man's pee instead."

"I'm so sorry, Six. It seems you need some rest. You should take a vacation to somewhere like Hokkaido. Rest up in the great outdoors and come back refreshed in body and soul."

As Lilith stares at me with eyes full of genuine pity, I explain myself.

"…I see you're getting involved in nonsense as usual. I mean, how the hell did you even convince Tiger Man to cooperate?"

Hey now, no need to look at me like I'm stupid.

"He made a fuss about it, so I told him it was under your orders."

"And you wonder why my reputation is so bad! It's all your fault! Also, the reason Tiger Man's urine works is because its properties instinctively incite fear on a bestial level, like territorial marking. Mine wouldn't have the same effect."

Lilith glares suspiciously at me as she backs away.

"Well, we won't know for sure until we try. Only losers never try."

"Shut up! Why do you only get motivated over weird things like this? That's not your character type! Also, I'm totally telling Astaroth about this."

Snow seems a little put off by our discussion, but then she grows contemplative.

"...Well, the suggestion sounds like the ramblings of a moron, but it might be worth a try."

"I thought the only idiots on this rock were our Combat Agents, but I guess I was wrong. I swear, everyone around me is a hopeless moron!"

"Since even Snow is suggesting we try it, why not just take one for the team, Lady Lilith? We'll look the other way."

Lilith's tentacles writhe beneath her lab coat as she tries to intimidate me.

"No, the idea I said was worth trying is using the waste of powerful monsters."

Lilith and I just exchange a glance after hearing Snow's calm explanation.

5

The Sand King, a giant mole that lives in the desert.

The Forest King, a giant lizard that, according to Snow, lives in the woods near our hideout.

Apparently, there's also a giant monster that rules this planet's skies...

"Hold on there, Snow. I get from your description that this 'Sky

King' is an impressive creature. I also understand that the scent of such a beast's pee would definitely terrify most other monsters, but…"

Lilith's expression becomes serious.

"I'm a scientist, not a Combat Agent. Sure, as a Supreme Leader, I can fight, but this sounds a bit outside my wheelhouse."

"Stop making excuses, Lady Lilith. If you can take out this Whatever King, we can start developing the land around here. This is the time for our Supreme Leader to show us why she's fit to lead."

Leaving the city of Grace, we're now making our way across the barren wastelands.

"Heh, I've got pretty sharp ears, you know. I've already heard the rumors. Lady Lilith's powers have put settling the Cursed Forest in reach. Not only that, but I've also heard she defeated countless monsters and savages single-handedly…"

I have no idea where she got this information, but Snow rattles off her knowledge with a cocky smile.

"I've seen glimpses of your many talents, Lady Lilith. No doubt with your power, we could even defeat the Great Beasts…"

"Well, sure, I probably could. I'm a Supreme Leader, after all. I may be the least suited for combat out of all the Supreme Leaders, but based on its name, it's a flying monster, right? Then it's a perfect target for my specialty: ranged attacks. But I hardly think gathering its pee should be my job."

"Could you quit bellyaching and just get it done, Lady Lilith? Look, I'll give you this golden beetle I found on this planet."

"In that case, I'm willing to give you this orange mokemoke hatchling. I captured it in the woods, thinking it'd be worth a fortune to a collector."

The beetle I show her draws Lilith's interest, but she's still less than enthusiastic.

"Just what do you take me for anyway? I mean, the beetle and the crawfish are interesting, so I'll take them, but I feel like you're trying to bribe me... Besides, we were originally discussing technology transfers. How did that turn into me fighting a giant monster? As I keep telling you, I'm a scientist. I'm a researcher. Neither are the same as a Combat Agent."

An unusual trinket or two is usually enough to mollify her, but she's being awfully contentious today.

"Lady Lilith, you're a huge fan of *Monster Panda*, right? This is just like the giant-monster-hunting quests in the game. The only difference is that we're doing it in real life. C'mon, Lady Lilith, come hunt with me."

......

"Hunting quest... Hunting quest..."

Lilith the Gamer takes the bait.

I just need one more push.

"Based on the name, I bet the Sky King's a dragon! Don't you want to see a dragon? The thing you killed in the forest was a lizard, but this time, it'll be an actual dragon. I mean, why don't we take out this Sky King or whatever and become dragonslayers?"

"Dragonslayer... Dragon... Dragon..."

Lilith's eyes brighten.

"A 23mm antiaircraft gun for Six, a heat-seeking missile launcher for me..."

As Lilith begins planning for an aerial battle against the yet-unknown monster...

"Six, I don't mean to complain when I'm the one who got Lady Lilith so fired up about this, but what are you scheming? You're being awfully cooperative today."

"There's a dangerous, giant monster hiding out in the skies around here, right? Then we should use the opportunity to get her to take it out. Otherwise, it'll become my *problem sooner or later."*

Yes. Now that I'm aware of this dangerous thing's existence, I'm almost positive that someone's eventually gonna ask me to kill it.

If I've learned anything, it's that it's best to nip potential problems in the bud as soon as possible.

"Well, it's technically the Guardian Beast of this kingdom, so I can't have you killing it...but still, if there's a battle, there's a chance that highly valuable Sky King feathers would get scattered around the area. And that would be..."

As Snow struggles to deal with her inner turmoil, I'm starting to figure out why she raised this idea.

However...

"Guardian Beast, huh...?"

I feel like we might be courting some sort of divine punishment by hunting a creature this revered...

"Six! Once we're dragonslayers, let's go meet those Dragon Squad Whatever Rangers whose names I can never remember. Then we can taunt them and tell them, *Dragon Squad, huh? That's a cool name. Well, but we've actually killed a real dragon.*"

"You realize doing things like that is why you skyrocketed to the top of the Heroes' most wanted list, right?"

I let out a weak laugh as Lilith enthusiastically holds up her fist.

There are a lot of problems having Lilith as a Supreme Leader, but so long as I'm with her, I don't have to worry about losing.

6

"Liar! Six, you're a liar! Dragonslayer my ass! That's a sparrow! That's just an overgrown sparrow!"

"Don't blame me, it's this planet's ecosystem that's screwed up. But the important thing is the bird poop. Could you hurry up and gather it?"

The Sky King is a sparrow.

A really, really big sparrow.

It's so big, it makes the griffin I fought look small.

"This isn't right. The aerodynamics wouldn't work if you scaled a sparrow to that size!"

"Please stop rambling and hurry up with the poop sample. Lady Lilith, as a scientist, you must be good at gathering samples, right?"

The giant sparrow hops around the wasteland, pecking at the ground with its beak.

"What do we do, Six? I can't exterminate a sparrow! When I was little, I picked up a weakened sparrow and nursed it back to health… I've had an attachment to them ever since…"

"You're a Supreme Leader of an evil organization! You're not supposed to be so cute and sentimental! That's not gonna win you any cool-boss points!"

Lilith and I are hiding behind a random boulder, arguing while watching the sparrow from a distance.

"Hey, Six, the Sky King is known for its curiosity. Why don't Lady Lilith and I go gather the Sky King's droppings while you draw its attention?"

Snow, the only one unfazed by the giant bird, pitches her plan.

"Yeah, no. That plan will get me eaten for sure. Your fancy head of snow-white hair would be way better for drawing its attention. I'll do the dirty work of gathering the poop, so go be a knight for once."

"No, no, I can't possibly let my commander do something as filthy as gathering bird waste. This sort of dirty work is something for the rank and file. You should have the honor of acting as bait."

……

"Hey, that reminds me. Why are you, of all people, so eager to go digging through poop? Do people pay tons of money for Sky King poop or something?"

"O-of course not! I've no ulterior motives! I've been learning about science from Alice while helping her. Yes, that's it. I'm work-ing to fulfill my scientific curiosity! I just want to poke around the Sky King's poop. I have no other motives!"

"Would you two cut it out with all this poop talk? Poop this and pee that. You sound like a pair of ten-year-olds."

Lilith's voice is thick with exasperation, but I actually think her comment is pretty insulting to ten-year-olds. I'm pretty sure they're a lot smarter than that.

"Tch, we're just wasting time arguing. I'll go draw its attention, so you two better grab its poop. If it's valuable, we're splitting the profits!"

"Okay, leave it to me! Oh, just so we're clear, the droppings them-selves don't have any value. However, it's possible we might find some valuables buried in them."

Based on Snow's description, I assume that means various shiny objects.

"*Sigh*, can't you two phrase it a little better...?"

I leave behind a muttering Lilith and start running toward the Sky King.

"The Sky King likes shiny objects! If you've got something valu-able, use it to draw the bird's attention!"

"Yo, over here, birdbrain! Look at this!"

As I step out from my hiding spot, the Sky King stops pecking at the ground and turns to look at me.

"It's the giant golden beetle I found in the Cursed Forest! If you want this, you better—"

"Heeeeey, what the heck are you doing?! That's *my* beetle!"

Despite Lilith's ambivalence when I first offered it to her, it looks like she's grown attached to the beetle, and she lets out a shrilled objection.

Captivated by the shimmering golden insect, the Sky King locks its gaze onto my hand.

I gently place the beetle at the Sky King's feet...

...and watch it promptly devour my offering in a single bite.

"Now!"

"What do you mean, 'now'?! It ate it! It just ate my precious beetle!"

As we speak, the poor bug is becoming acquainted with the Sky King's stomach.

"Six, when I said shiny things, I meant jewels and precious metals!" yells Snow as she edges toward the Sky King.

"In that case, leave it to me! Look at thiiiiis!"

Learning my lesson from the loss of my golden beetle, I pull out something shiny the Sky King won't gobble up.

It's my prized possession: the necklace I bought to placate a certain clingy disaster who's been begging me for a new one.

I feel like it's brimming with the accumulated wrath of a vengeful spinster, but with this...!

I swing Grimm's necklace around to draw the Sky King's attention...

"Chirp."

"Oh."

Instead of the necklace, the Sky King grabs *me*.

"...Lady Lilith, it seems this is it for me. Working at Kisaragi was awful and abusive, but still, I had fun here and there. Please give my regards to Lady Astaroth and Lady Belial..."

"Don't give up! Hang on, Six, I'll shoot that thing down, and..."

"Wait, Lady Lilith! The Sky King is a Guardian Beast! I can't have you slaying it!"

"Chirp!"

Gripped in the Sky King's talons, I'm carried high into the air.

7

"…This is Combat Agent Six. Lady Lilith, can you hear me? Over."

"This is Lilith, and yes, I can hear you. We tracked you part of the way using the satellite-link system, but we lost you around the rocky area. Where are you, exactly? Over."

Having been dragged off by the Sky King…

"Right now, I'm in the Sky King's nest. Looks like Snow was right about its nature. It hasn't attacked me yet."

…I'm currently in its lair.

"Lady Lilith, this is pretty impressive. There's tons of shiny stuff here."

The bird's nest I'm in is overflowing with glimmering objects.

I can see a wide assortment of gems and an enormous pile of gold coins.

There are also magic swords and glowing armor poking out of the heap.

"Six, I'd like to hear more about the shiny stuff. Then again, it's probably just junk a bird would collect. Glass beads and pretty rocks, right?" asks Lilith, trying to convince herself that the sparrow hasn't actually collected anything of real value.

"There's a ton of jewels and gold coins. Also, there's piles of things that look like magic swords…"

After delivering my report, I hear a brief, muffled response from Lilith, and an oddly polite Snow calls back.

"Commander, can you hear me? It is I, your loyal subordinate Snow. I am relieved to hear you are safe. When you were taken from us, I felt an ache in my heart for your safety…"

Who the hell are you?

"Hey! Give me back my radio and don't butt in! But yeah, we're glad you're all right… So, Six, do you know where you are? I'll come fetch you myself."

......

"I don't know where I am exactly, but it's somewhere between some cliffs. I'm about to request some rope so I can climb down on my own, so you don't need to come get me."

""We can't have that!""

My boss's and my subordinate's voices overlap.

"...There's some Sky King droppings in the corner. I'll collect a bit and head back."

The Sky King is curled up in the back of the lair, having lost all interest in me the moment I let it keep the necklace.

Doesn't look like it'll attack when I leave.

"Hold on, Six, forget the droppings for now. Instead, let's look into these shiny treasures..."

"Do you have any idea how rare an opportunity it is to be able to enter the Sky King's lair?! Don't you dare leave that nest empty-handed! Forget about the poop and grab a few magic swords!"

Forgetting the whole reason we're here, my boss and my subordinate focus on their greed.

"I'm not taking that stuff at a time like this. It won't mind me pilfering some droppings, but it'll come after me if I make off with any of its precious treasures."

I glance over at the Sky King. It's taken a real shine to the necklace and is now using its beak to toy with it.

"What sort of cowardly excuse is that?! Leaving behind treasure that's just sitting in front of you—what sort of adventurer are you?!"

"Ma'am, I'm a Combat Agent."

Hearing that, Snow throws insults in my direction.

"Lady Lilith is right! To sneak into the Sky King's lair and acquire its haul—that's the sort of adventure story every man dreams of! And you're going to throw away that opportunity?!"

Sky King? Adventure? It's a giant sparrow.

It'd be a different story if I was in the lair of an actual dragon.

Ignoring the two yelling at me over the radio, I shovel some poop into a bag...

"Six, don't you leave! We should be close now!"

"I won't leave you to face danger alone, Commander! If we must die, we'll die together!"

With their goals completely changed, the duo yells with ragged breath...

I mean, these two are just getting in the way.

If they make it to the lair, I bet they're gonna make my escape harder.

As I struggle to figure out a way to convince them to back off, the Sky King raises its head.

I don't know why, but the damn thing is still toying with the necklace I was planning to give Grimm...

"...Combat Agent Six to Alice at headquarters. I'm in a weird situation. Think you can gimme a hand with those smarts of yours, partner? Over!"

A necklace falls from the lair atop the cliff.

As it hurtles down toward Lilith's head, she grabs it out of the air with one of her tentacles.

"Hmm, is this...?"

"Isn't that the necklace that bastard showed the Sky King earlier...?"

The Sky King left the lair to look for food, so I retrieved the necklace and tossed it at Lilith.

Evidently figuring out that I dropped it, Lilith holds the necklace up to the light and glances skyward.

"Six, can you hear me? A necklace just fell on top of me. You're nearby, right?"

"Combat Agent Six here. That's correct, Lady Lilith. I'm above you. The Sky King should be coming back soon, so if you could buy me some time, that'd be great."

""What?""

As Lilith and Snow wail in unison, they're swallowed up by a giant shadow.

The Sky King, now with a full belly, has returned to its nest.

Before it lands, it catches sight of the necklace that Lilith's holding up to the light...

"Chirp, chirp, chirp!"

"Who the heck was it who said the Sky King was gentle?! It's super hostile!"

"Lady Lilith, it wants the shiny object! The necklace you're holding! It's after that!"

As Lilith risks life and limb acting as bait, I stuff as many coins and Sky King feathers as possible into my backpack.

But it's not quite time to climb down the rope.

It'll be a problem if the decoys leave me behind, so I egg on their greed.

"Lady Lilith, I'll drop you some of the Sky King's treasure hoard."

Warning the decoys, I grab the remaining gems next and toss them toward the ground.

"Well done, Six! Good work! Grrr, damned bird! Now that it's on the ground, this treasure is free for the taking! Get lost!"

"Bwa-ha-ha-ha-ha-ha-ha! Ah-ha-ha-ha-ha-ha-ha!"

Glancing down from my perch, I see Lilith guarding against the Sky King's pecking while stepping on gems with her foot and slowly pulling them toward her.

As for Snow, she's cackling as she crawls around on the ground, gathering up gems in both arms.

"Chirp, chirp, chirp!"

"Evil organizations are pillars of avarice! We can't back down to a mere bird with this much loot in plain sight!"

"A wonderful attitude, Lady Lilith! I will not back down! Even against a Guardian Beast!"

With the two of them caught up grabbing the treasure raining down from above...

"This is Combat Agent Six. I'm returning to base. Got plenty of souvenirs for you. Over."

"Yep, good work. Try not to get caught up with the decoys. Over."

Gathering up the poop and the backpack, I sneak away from the area.

8

Having recovered the loot and the poop, I return to our temporary headquarters in the park.

"Tch, that was awful... I usually prefer staying in. This is the last time we're doing that, okay...?"

With the pockets of her lab coat bulging with gems, Lilith flops onto the grass, muttering complaints.

I returned on my own, and Lilith, unable to attack the Sky King, appears to have jammed as many gems as she could into her pockets and fled.

"What happened to Snow?"

"...The Sky King hauled her away when she refused to drop her loot. Since your rope's still tied to the nest, I'm sure it'll let her go when she gives up on the treasure."

I can't imagine that greedy woman coming home empty-handed, so it doesn't look like we'll see her again for a while.

After lying on the ground for a bit, Lilith sits up. Alice is there, shirking her hideout-construction duties apparently, so Lilith calls to her.

"Alice, lend me a hand here, will you? We're going to start on pesticide development."

Gazing into a bucket a short distance away, Alice doesn't even bother looking at her when responding.

"Yeah, welcome back or whatever, Lady Lilith. Right now, I'm busy with my orange-crawfish observations, so if you need help with one of your useless ideas, check back later."

"It's not useless! And hey, that's *my* crawfish! I got it in exchange for my work!"

Alice seems focused on the small mokemoke Snow's been keeping.

"Alice, do you know how this country meets its food needs? It's fascinating. They use hydroponics inside factories."

"I knew that."

"Isn't that surprising?! And the reason for that is…"

Lilith freezes after Alice responds without taking her eyes off the bucket.

"The farms are getting attacked by flying monsters, yeah? I've known that for ages and have been working on methods to change that inefficient model."

……

"…Wait, hold on a minute. Really? Well then, let me hear what you've come up with."

Aware that our day's labor may go to waste, Lilith waits with sweat trickling down her brow.

"This planet's monsters seem to have a habit of avoiding places that smell like powerful creatures. This is why I forced Tiger Man to give up some of his pee…"

"Again with the pee?! Why are you all so obsessed with organic waste?!"

I try to cheer Lilith up as she holds her head and screams.

"Calm down, Lady Lilith. I mean, you're still technically a Supreme Leader and an upstanding lady. You shouldn't be saying 'pee' over and over."

"I'm not repeating it because I want to! ...So did it work?"

Alice finally looks up from the bucket.

"No, Tiger Man's pee didn't have much of an effect. But waste from a stronger creature should solve that problem... Hey, Lady Lilith, could you come over and fill this bucket with...?"

"Not another word! Here. Use the stuff Six brought back."

Interrupting Alice, Lilith snatches the bag from my hands and holds it out.

"Alice, use this to complete the development of the pesticide. In the meantime, I'll..."

Lilith then reaches into her pockets and takes out some glittering gems...

"Mwa-ha-ha-ha-ha-ha-ha! Look, Six! Gems! And they're gems I've never even seen on Earth! No doubt they'll be worth a fortune if I take them back home..."

"Those are glass orbs you can find just lying on the ground around here. They look different because of the difference in atmospheric composition, but they'll return to ordinary glass the moment you take them back to Earth."

Lilith throws the rock in her hand.

"H-how can that be?! Alice, try appraising the other rocks. I'm sure there's at least one that's worth a lot..."

"No, they're all pretty much worthless... Oh, hey, this one's a tourmaline. At this size, you can sell it for about three hundred yen."

After Alice finishes her appraisal, Lilith falls to her knees.

Ignoring her, I take out the coins and Sky King feathers I stuffed into my backpack.

"I brought gold coins and shed feathers as souvenirs. Snow claims the feathers can be sold for a pretty penny."

"Good work, partner. I'll keep the feathers for research and handle the coins. I'll use them to do some investments and trading, so lemme know when you're short on money."

Whoo-hoo! Guess I'm drinkin' tonight!

…Lilith enviously watches our exchange, muttering to herself.

"Hey, Alice, aren't you pampering Six a bit too much? I'm your creator. I'll lend you some money, so could you use your information sources to—?"

"Do it yourself."

…Looks like Alice really is in a rebellious phase. She coldly dismisses Lilith without a second thought.

CHAPTER 3

🐾 Vs. the Mud King

1

It's been three days since we got a sample of the Sky King's droppings.

"Congratulations, Lady Lilith! You finally accomplished something on this planet."

"Hold on. This isn't my first accomplishment. I mean, I killed that giant lizard in the forest, remember? I also found that mysterious subterranean facility."

Once they were treated with Alice's specially developed pesticide, the formerly defenseless vegetables stopped attracting flying monsters.

Since there's a limited number of those mysterious concrete structures around the kingdom, farming open land will allow for a substantial increase in food production.

Once the supply of vegetables and grains goes up, they can start raising larger domesticated animals.

Which means there won't be a need to cannibalize sentient creatures that can speak human languages.

Even though I've tried to avoid it myself, I still can't get over watching others eat orc meat.

I'm not a fan of critiquing the customs of others, but this is one food culture I'd be happy to see end.

"You know, my work here's been a lot duller than I imagined. I was hoping for something more like…dramatically improving the quality of life with the power of science or making the natives panic using a bit of superior technology…"

The Lilithification and Praise Project that was supposed to progress by way of tech transfers and getting the local ruling power in our pocket isn't going as hoped.

And that's partly due to…

"Not a whole lot we can do about it, Lady Lilith. Sure, this planet's science is primitive, but they've got magic to make up for it."

"That's the problem! Magic, shmagic! They're just spitting in the face of science at this point!"

It's understandable that Lilith would fly into a rage much like Alice does.

Part of the reason behind this kingdom's undeveloped technology is something called "magitech."

One example of this is the water spirit stones, which are exported by our neighbor-turned-enemy, the kingdom of Toris.

Evidently, they're used to pay water spirits in exchange for having them bring water from somewhere else.

…Yes, you heard that right. Water spirits.

"What the hell are these spirits anyway?! There's a limit to this fantasy-world nonsense! When I tried to show off my lighter to a local, they laughed and said fire spirit stones are more useful. The heck is a fire spirit stone?!"

"Well, it's not like magic is all-powerful. When I asked my subordinate Grimm to create some pretty women, she told me to bugger off."

At that moment, Lilith scrunches her face into a grimace at the mention of Grimm's name.

"Grimm... Grimm, right... That's the shady woman you mentioned in your reports, right?"

"I mean, if you want to call her that, I guess she's kind of shady, but I think she'd cry if she heard. I mean, you're the one who wears a lab coat all year long."

Just then.

<Evil Points Acquired>

"...Huh."

"...Six, did you just get some Evil Points?"

Seeing my surprised reaction, Lilith inquires with a similar expression.

In fact, the points just keep coming, and the announcements become a steady rhythm in my head.

"Yeah, I did get a random notification, and the points are still pouring in, actually. Is this happening to you as well, Lady Lilith?"

"Yeah, I keep getting points... I wonder what's going on. It's creepy not knowing the cause..."

Even as we tilt our heads in puzzlement, the announcements don't stop.

If we just leave things the way they are, my point deficit will be gone in no time.

"The weird thing is we're both getting them. What did you do this time, Lady Lilith?"

"Wait, that's my line. I don't think I've done anything notable on this planet, so it might be something back in Japan. Maybe the fact that I'm here flirting with you got back to Astaroth, and her heartbreak is being counted as an act of villainy?"

I don't think our super-*tsundere* leader is quite that cute...

"I wonder if there's snooping equipment installed here or something. Do you wanna try flirting some more?"

"Nope, I'm going to have to decline… Hey, watch where you put those hands! If you've got sexual harassment on the brain, I've got ways of dealing with that."

My grabby hands recoil from Lilith.

"Commander, we've got a problem! There's a chance a Demon Lord operative found their way into the city!"

With those words, the aforementioned Grimm appears in the room.

Leaving behind her wheelchair, Grimm approaches us by walking barefoot on the park's grass.

"…Hmm? What's going on, Commander? I leave you alone for a bit, and you use that time to see another girl? You don't look like you'd be that popular, yet somehow, you keep meeting new people!"

Displeasure plain on her face, Grimm glares at Lilith, who's standing next to me.

I wave my hand at the little scientist.

"This is my boss, Lady Lilith. She's one of Kisaragi's Supreme Leaders!"

"Oh?!"

Hearing that, Grimm holds a hand to her mouth as though she's figured something out, then straightens her posture…

"A pleasure to make your acquaintance, Lady Lilith. I am Grimm Grimoire, Combat Agent Six's fiancée. No doubt I have much to learn, but I appreciate your instruction and mentorship."

Sitting down on the park lawn, Grimm bows formally to Lilith.

"…Six, a moment please."

Lilith gestures for me to join her.

I approach as instructed…

"What's this about her being your fiancée? Did you really get engaged to a native of this planet? What about all the flirting you were doing with Astaroth on Earth? What's the meaning of this?"

"She's not my fiancée. We just made a promise that if we're both single in ten years, we'd marry each other. Besides, I never really flirted with Lady Astaroth..."

"That's literally an engagement! And yes, you were flirting with Astaroth!"

Glancing over at Grimm, I see she's watching our whispered conversation with a smile on her face, her hands folded over her stomach.

Lilith looks less than pleased as she approaches Grimm.

"Well, fine, I guess I'll introduce myself at the very least... My name's Lilith. I'm one of the Kisaragi Corporation's Supreme Leaders. I'm the mother to all Combat Agents and mutants, Lilith the Black! I've known this man for a long time; we're practically family. Seems you've done much for our Six."

Lilith speaks with her hands stuffed in her pockets while glaring up at Grimm.

As for Grimm herself, she doesn't seem particularly bothered by the fact that my boss is acting like some random gangster.

"Not at all, Mother! In fact, it is I who owes Sir Six!"

"Seriously, it's such a chore to push you around in your wheelchair and carry you up and down various obstacles. Not to mention that you die every time I turn my head."

Grimm puffs out her cheeks at my words, but I find that sort of affectation irritating from a woman her age.

In contrast to the cheerful Grimm, Lilith mutters to herself, face frozen in shock.

"...Huh? D-did you just...call me 'Mother'?"

Ignoring her stunned mother-in-law, Grimm keeps puffing out her cheeks as she responds:

"I mean, even if you say that, it's not like I can help it. I can't wear shoes, after all. I mean, I feel plenty bad for making you do it. That's why I pay for dinner all the time, since you're always short on money anyway."

"Those two things are separate, you know. I mean, I use the allowance Alice gives me to pay for things all the time. Also, stop inflating your cheeks like that. It's not cute when a hag does it. It's just annoying."

I guess I crossed a line with the word *hag*. I end up having to defend myself as Grimm tries to strangle me. While this plays out, Lilith mutters to herself again.

"Hey... Did you really just call me 'Mother'...?"

Leaving the flummoxed Lilith to one side, Grimm bares her fangs and snarls.

"Speaking of which, Commander, why do you even accept an allowance from Alice?! *I'm* the only woman you should depend on! When we're married, I'll spoil you rotten!"

Suddenly, it seems like marrying Grimm wouldn't be the worst idea, but the sense of danger that I've honed over years working as a Combat Agent advises me otherwise.

"That's honestly tempting, but didn't you have a reason for being here?"

Remembering her original purpose, Grimm returns to her senses.

"That's right, this is hardly the time to be calmly exchanging greetings! Seems there's a Demon Lord operative inside the city, just like during the Undead Festival!"

Lilith and I exchange glances at the word *operative*.

"...Well, we can't let that go unanswered! Terrorism and sabotage ops are our bread and butter. Just leave it to us!"

"Well, if I must, since you always buy me dinner... But you better pay for our drinks tonight."

Having secured our assistance, Grimm smiles as though reassured.

2

And so, led by Grimm...

"Issue the evacuation order! Fire's effective against the Mud King! Once the residents are safe, bring all the fire spirit stones you can find!"

"Oil! Spread some oil! The Mud King is intelligent. If it sees oil, it'll steer clear to avoid the fire!"

...we arrive to a spectacle of utter pandemonium and freeze.

"Lady Lilith, I have a really bad feeling about this."

"What a coincidence, Six. I was just thinking of turning around and going home."

That black slime is now crawling out of the dry well where Lilith had left the drilling equipment running a few days ago.

"...Pretty sure this one's on you, Lady Lilith."

"Wait, Six, it's too early to jump to conclusions. I think we should carefully investigate the facts before announcing any findings."

Both Lilith and I had completely forgotten about the drilling equipment until now.

If it was up to me, I'd just feign ignorance and go watch the crawfish back at the base.

But...

"Lady Lilith, my Evil Points haven't stopped since earlier."

"Oh really. Then it seems this counts as your crime, too. Good work, Six. This is quite the act of villainy!"

......

"Oh no you don't. You're not pinning this all on me, you bowl-cut lab rat! You're getting Evil Points, too! What do we do about this?! We're gonna end up owing Tillis again!"

"Oh yeah? Are you saying this is my fault?! Fine, it's my fault! I'm a Supreme Leader of an evil organization! I spread destruction and chaos without even thinking about it! I'm sooooo sorry that I'm such a charismatic, shining example of villainy!"

"You're choosing to lash out at me now?! I called you here for reinforcements, and all you've done is add to our headaches! You utterly useless boss! Quit plugging your ears and try denying it! I DARE YOU!"

As I rack my brains for a way to deal with this blame-shifting geek, Grimm looks over at us with her head tilted quizzically.

"Hey, what are you two arguing about? As you can see, that's the Mud King. We're going to calm it down, so could you help us out?"

Based on the fact that Grimm's using this "Mud King" term we've been hearing since earlier, it seems she knows about the slime.

"What's the Mud King? Is it related to that black stuff?"

"Oh, right, I keep forgetting you're not from around here, Commander. That black slime, the Mud King, is a giant monster sealed underneath the Grace Kingdom. It's why this country's always short on water."

...Wait, what?

"Hey, um, does everyone in the kingdom know about this?"

"Well, not everyone. Ordinary citizens don't. I mean, knowing this thing is sealed under their feet isn't exactly going to help them go about their daily lives."

Still, if that thing's there, why didn't Snow warn us...?

And it didn't seem like she knew what this black slime was...

"Still, aside from blabbermouths, idiots, or people who might sell the information for money, almost everyone who serves the kingdom knows about it. Keep that in mind, okay, Commander?"

"Ohhh, I get it now."

Which means a certain idiot who is also extremely easy to bribe wasn't let in on the secret.

…Just then.

"Combat Agent Six, this is our time to shine. I've already ordered the quick-drying cement. Let's shove that troublesome slime back underground. We can worry about finding the culprit once that's done."

"Roger, Lady Lilith. No doubt this is all the fault of the Demon Lord's Army's Heine of the Flames! Now that I think about it, she also infiltrated the city in a stuffed-animal suit during the Undead Festival!"

"I see! While I've never met that woman, if you say it's her fault, then that must be the case. Damned Demon Lord's Army! They'll pay for this…!"

At our enthusiastic denunciation of the evil Demon Lord's Army, Grimm eyes us with a puzzled look on her face.

<Evil Points Acquired>

One hour later.

"What the heck is up with this planet?! I heard it was primitive and had no modern weaponry, but that's not true at all…! I, a Supreme Leader, damn near got the ero-game treatment from an overgrown amoeba!"

Lilith fumes after burying the Mud King—and the incriminating drill—under the quick-drying cement.

As it turns out, her mechanical tentacles aren't suited to fending off gelatinous creatures like slimes, and after being thoroughly drenched in its gloopy residue, she slumps over in exhaustion.

"The reports didn't lie. It's just that there's some ridiculous things from time to time, but the base level is still really weak. I mean, we Combat Agents can handle most monsters with ease."

With various parts of her outfit thoroughly soaked through with black slime, Lilith rages as Grimm gently wipes the little tyrant's face with a handkerchief.

"I feel like I'm getting hit with every ridiculous thing out there. The giant lizard in the woods, the Sky King, and now this Mud King. I can't help but think you're using me to deal with all these overpowered problem characters."

Seems she's got enough smarts to notice that pattern.

"Please cheer up, Mother. Your help was invaluable."

"You just called me 'Mother' again! I won't overlook it this time! Why do you keep calling me that?! I'm Six's boss, not his actual mom! You can't just claim me as your mother-in-law!"

The motherly figure—who's younger than I am—finally lets the complaints fly.

"But, Mother!"

"Stop saying 'Mother'!"

Because of her small stature, Lilith, who's getting her face wiped with a towel, looks more like the daughter than the mother.

"What the heck is wrong with your subordinates, Six?! The Chimera girl ends up being a boy; the devout paladin, who should be ripe for corruption, ends up being morally bankrupt from the jump; and then there's this man-stealer who uses a wheelchair despite the fact that she can walk! I know Kisaragi has no shortage of colorful characters among our ranks, but this kingdom's people are just as awful…"

To be fair, the Chimera dude isn't even my subordinate.

"Please hold a moment, Lady Superior. There's a reason for my wheelchair! It's because I suffered the backlash from a curse when I fought my greatest rival…"

Grimm's use of the word *curse* catches Lilith's attention.

"Curse, huh…? I saw it in the reports, but Alice claims it's just a form of hypnosis."

"Please don't listen to that reality-denying brat! I mean, just the other day, while I was chatting with a spectral acquaintance of mine, Alice brought this weird device over and tried to suck up the ghost."

The "odd device" in question was a vacuum cleaner.

Oh yes. Inspired by an old movie, Alice started carrying a vacuum cleaner on her back and claiming she was going hoax-busting.

…Grimm seems to notice Lilith's skeptical gaze and hurriedly offers a defense.

"Wait, I've seen that look before! It's the same as that brat's! The look of a skeptic! …Fine. Since we've managed to stave off the Demon Lord's Army's evil scheme to release the Mud King…I'll show you, Commander, and Lady Superior, what I do in my spare time!" says Grimm, a confident smile on her lips.

3

That night.

Following Grimm, Lilith and I walk through a back alley on the edge of the city.

"Hey, Grimm. Isn't this where the weird guys and loose ladies live? I think I'm getting a pretty good idea of how you usually pass the time…"

"Commander! Why, I never! No, it's nothing like that. I mean, you're right that this is more or less a slum of sorts. But we're heading for the noble district. It's quickest to cut through here."

Each time we pass the scantily clad ladies on the roadside, they wink and blow kisses in my direction, but Grimm tightens her grip on my arm in a show of possessiveness.

"…This is a place riddled with dive bars, where women of the night peddle their services. This is also where many people who've lost their homes turn. It is the dark underbelly of this kingdom, in a manner of speaking…"

Grimm says all this with a certain darkness creeping into her expression. She then quietly lays a gold coin next to a slumbering homeless man's head.

When her presence wakes him, Grimm offers up a gentle smile.

The homeless man picks up the coin, then looks from Grimm to me and then back to Grimm...

"Oh, good to see you again, bud. You givin' me some spending money?"

"Hey, old man. This is one of my subordinates, but it looks like she wants to give you an allowance. Go ahead and take it."

Witnessing the exchange between the homeless man and me, Grimm and Lilith direct a slack-jawed stare at us.

"Anyway, I gotta go. Take care of yourself, old man. It's getting cold out here at night. If you're gonna sleep, you oughta do it at home."

"Eh, I used up my old lady's savings, so I been stuck out here for a bit. I heard you've been sleeping in the park, bud. Don't catch a cold, eh?"

As the "homeless" man speaks with a smile, he grasps the coin Grimm gave him and wanders off.

"...So, Commander... You and that homeless fellow know each other?"

"He's just a random old dude I bump into around here from time to time. Sometimes, we share a drink. He's got a bit of a gambling problem, and his wife kicks him out of the house every few days when he spends too much money."

Before I finish, Grimm speeds up in her wheelchair.

"You there! If you have a home and a wife, give me back my money, you wretched bum! Don't go napping in an alley if you're not actually homeless!"

As he notices Grimm's approach, the man quickly scrambles over a wall and disappears. Watching all this, Lilith sighs in my general direction.

"Six, I feel like I've been saying this a lot, but you really should choose your subordinates and friends better."

That's not really all that convincing coming from a Supreme Leader of an evil organization.

After watching the not-so-homeless man depart, we continue walking until Grimm brings us to...

"Is this really a noble's estate? It says sale pending..."

...a fancy-looking building just past the slums that certainly seems like it belongs to rich people.

Lilith reads off the letters on the sign, but I can't tell what it says.

Alice's translation only works for sound.

She told me to learn to read the country's writing on my own.

Considering that I still struggle to read and write English, I think asking me to learn the language of a completely different world is expecting a bit much.

That's the sort of task best left to my brainy partner.

"This estate once belonged to the man who served as the army's chief of staff. Remember when the Demon Lord's Army attacked the city? The chief of staff at the time suddenly announced his resignation and vanished one day. For a man who had earned that title to resign without warning...that's suspicious, right? A little bit after that, rumors started going around that his estate that had gone up for sale was haunted..."

Lilith nods along with interest at Grimm's explanation.

"I see. So you've come here to perform an exorcism? I love paranormal documentaries. It's so much fun to send a finely doctored photo to the program, then watch a bunch of shady weirdos lose their heads over it..."

Man, this chick is something else...

Though, in a way, this sort of petty villainy is something to be admired.

"Huh? Lady Lilith, Six, and Grimm? Can't say I saw this coming. What the hell are you all doing here?"

"Alice?! That's my line! Why do you always show up wherever I am?!"

Standing in front of us is the android who hates the supernatural and paranormal more than anything in creation.

I have no idea what she's planning to do at this time of night, but she's got a giant vacuum cleaner strapped to her back.

Alice turns to Grimm, who's gotten up out of her wheelchair.

"Ah, so we meet again, Scammer-1."

"Who the hell are you calling 'Scammer-1'?! I'm only going to ask one more time. Why are you here, Alice? Are you going to interrupt my work again?!"

She just said "again," didn't she? Is this common for Alice?

"You're the one who's interrupting my work. This estate's value is finally going down, thanks to my efforts. I'll take care of the ghost-busting myself, so you're welcome to go on home."

Grimm's expression is frozen in a look of irritation as Alice casually dismisses her before lowering the vacuum cleaner to the ground.

I have no idea what's going on here, but I'm glad my partner seems to be enjoying herself.

"Looks like you've had quite a bit fun while I wasn't around."

"Yeah, well, Scammer-1 here keeps disrupting my side gig of property flipping. The value of the chief of staff's house here is finally dropping after all the rumors I spread, making it ripe for purchase. As it happens, the famous Ghost Hunter Alice is here to take care of those very rumors."

"W-wait, what did you just say?! I thought you mentioned rumormongering…"

…Oh, I see.

I finally understand why Alice has been handing out candy to the kids around this neighborhood.

"Given your time with Kisaragi, I'm guessing you've figured out what I'm up to, right, Six?"

"Stop talking in riddles! Tell me what's going on!"

Lilith explains for Alice as Grimm continues to look confused.

"So to clarify, Alice trained some kids to go around saying they've seen shadows or blood-spattered men roaming houses that are for sale. Once the bad rumors have spread enough to lower the price..."

No one's going to believe it when a single child says they've seen a ghost.

But if multiple children start saying they've seen ghosts, well, it goes from a childish prank to a rumor...

Hearing that, Grimm cries out:

"You're running a scam!"

That's right. This is all just a page out of the Kisaragi handbook.

"Alice, don't you feel guilty putting children up to this?! And what an awful thing to do to the buyers you're targeting!"

Hearing Grimm's criticism, Alice responds with a wag of her finger.

"I'm only buying up properties from problematic sellers. Most of them are petty crooks like the chief of staff. Also, as for using children, as you can see, I'm an innocent child myself!"

"There's no way there are kids this conniving!"

Which is when I realize something else.

"Oh. If you're the source of the rumors, then you know there's no ghosts to bust, and you can pretend you have a perfect ghost-hunting record. So that's how you spun the story to gain renown as a ghost hunter."

"That about covers it. Oh, and while we're at it, I'm not telling the brats to lie. Lying children usually get caught anyway. Which is why I set up a projector ahead of time and use holograms to scare the kids I round up using candy as bait."

Lilith and I surround Alice and begin boisterously praising her.

"Clever! As expected of my partner! So very clever!"

"Well done, Alice! As expected of my creation!"

""Hail Alice! Hail Alice! Hail Alice!!""

"Could you stop with that 'Hail Alice' crap? It doesn't sound like a compliment."

Lilith and I pat the hell out of Alice's head.

"Seriously, knock it off! Oh, it's true... There's no undead presence here! *Sigh*, then why did I come out all this way...?"

Seeing Grimm fall to her knees, gazing up at the estate, Lilith feels a pang of guilt and turns to her.

"Alice, I'm a science absolutist as well, but couldn't you be a little more, I don't know, subtle about this? She's a subordinate of Kisaragi, right?"

"No offense, Lady Lilith, but this is a matter of my very existence. Fantasy crap like gods, demons, and spirits are all going to be busted by my hand."

As one created with the cutting edge in modern technology, Alice just can't accept the paranormal.

...All right.

"Lady Lilith, since I can't use Evil Points, could you get me a vacuum cleaner like the one Alice has?"

"What...? Are you planning to get involved in this idiocy, too? ...Fine. As your superior, I need to be involved as well. I'll order two vacuum cleaners—one for me and one for you, Six."

"Thank you, Lady Lilith! I knew I could count on you."

...As Lilith and I are equipping ourselves with the vacuum cleaners sent by HQ, Grimm comes to me in tears, pleading as she grabs me by the waist.

"Commander, I thought you were on my side! Please stop! Adults shouldn't be doing something this ridiculous!"

How rude. Lilith and I both love this sort of charade, so we're actually pretty excited.

Grimm seems to notice that Lilith and I are more than happy to take part.

"...Fine. In that case, I've got an idea of my own..."

Standing barefoot on the ground, Grimm glances up at the sky—

"Fortunately for me, today's a full moon. The perfect phase...just like when I accidentally summoned that demon..."

Grimm continues staring at the heavens, smiling as though confident of victory.

"The full moon has a special meaning for beings beyond the ken of humanity. I'm sick of being treated like some scam artist! I'm going to show this little brat what I'm capable of! I'll use my powers to summon a demon so impressively terrifying, you'll piss yourself on the spot!"

Declaring all that in a single breath, Grimm retrieves from her bosom a piece of paper with a magic circle drawn on it and spreads it out on the ground.

"Grimm, calm down! You never actually succeed when you say things like that!"

"I haven't known you long, but I know that making a grand declaration of that sort is practically jinxing yourself!"

Grimm snarls at Lilith and me as we express our concern for her.

"Silence! If that brat's existence centers around denying the supernatural, then mine is dedicated to beseeching the gods!"

Grimm gazes up at the full moon, folding her hands together as though in supplication and prayer.

"Yes, this is all that I have! This is all that is left to me! What else do I have...? Above-average looks and a deceptively curvy figure. And then there's all the money I have saved up for marriage, my homemaking abilities, and my deep, deep love and devotion reserved solely for that special someone!!"

Grimm, who seems to have much more to offer than her prayers, gazes up at the pale-gold moon, yelling out in anguish.

Unlike the words leaving her lips, her eyes turn as clear and innocent as a child's as she looks fervently to the sky—

"My name is Grimm Grimoire! At this point, I don't care if
they're not particularly handsome. I don't care if they don't have any
money. All I want is someone who will love me and only me! I want
to get married! If you can grant me this wish, I won't even care if it's a
demon or a dark god! If you will listen to my earnest desire, then hear
my call and be summoned to these lands!"

Despite the fact that, unlike last time, there's no sacrificial offer-
ings or anything, the magic circle glows with a piercing, white light.

It shines even brighter than when she summoned a demon, as if
sympathizing with the plight of a woman facing eternal spinsterhood.

"S-Six! Alice! What the heck is going on?! The reports claimed
she's a scam artist, but this doesn't look like cheap special effects or
holograms to me...!"

There's a hint of panic in Lilith's voice, and she deploys her tentacles from beneath her lab coat. The magic circle glows so brightly that
the neighboring houses begin stirring.

As the light fades, in response to the tragic plea of the spinster,
what appears is—

4

"Commander, what should I do...? My all-too-pure wish has summoned an angel, of all things..."

Given that she's describing her own wish as pure, it doesn't seem
like she feels *that* guilty about it.

"Well, I mean, you managed to show Alice and Lady Lilith your
power, and it's a lot better than summoning a demon or a ghost, isn't it?
I mean, she's pretty easy on the eyes, so what's the problem?"

Responding to Grimm's summons, an angel with snow-white hair and wings appears before us.

She gives off such a divine aura that the very act of looking upon her makes me want to confess and repent for my past sins.

Garbed in pure-white clothing, the angel has a shimmering halo of light floating above her head, and she scatters motes of light with every flap of her wings.

The angel, still unsure what to make of the situation, slowly surveys her surroundings.

Lilith, frozen in shock over the unprecedented development, stares wide-eyed at the angel.

"I don't know if it's good or bad, actually. You know I'm a follower of Zenarith, right? The other faiths treat her as though she's a dark god. I mean, I don't feel guilty about it, but I'm not sure an angel wouldn't judge me over it…"

"No, I'm pretty sure you're screwed. I mean, your faith's all about undeath and disaster, right? You summon ghosts and demons, so you're definitely in the *enemy of angels* camp. The whole nocturnal thing means you're on the side of darkness, duh."

Hearing this, Grimm cowers behind me.

Surprisingly, Lilith, who always pokes fun at this sort of supernatural stuff, also appears unsettled.

"What's wrong, Lady Lilith? You're the sort who'd pick your nose and shrug if God himself came down and started lecturing you, right?"

"What the hell, Six?! No, I wouldn't pick my nose. I mean, you can feel it, can't you? Aren't your instincts telling you that thing isn't something humanity should be insulting…?"

The angel looks like a winged woman with almost frighteningly beautiful features.

She strikes me as a calm, cool beauty, but she's not doing much. She's just floating in place.

"…I mean, you've been shivering, too."

At the frightened Lilith's words, I finally notice my trembling legs.

Oh, so this is what fearful reverence feels like.

I doubt any living creature could do anything other than kneel in supplication at the angel's feet.

As proof, Grimm, who is ordinarily a bit pale, is now white as a sheet, and she wears the expression of someone facing certain doom.

What do I do? Maybe if I try worshipping her, I'll receive a blessing or something.

"What a thing to summon! Sheesh!"

"How was I supposed to know an angel would pop out of the summoning circle?! It just means my wishes were that pure!"

Despite the fact that she's probably in the most danger from a religious point of view, Grimm still seems to have a shred of composure.

"Anyway, Six, since we don't know if it can speak or not, let's try to get it to leave while doing our absolute best not to offend it."

Grimm and I nod at Lilith's suggestion.

Just then, I'm reminded there's someone here who is completely unaffected by this sort of supernatural event.

"Hey, why the hell are you wearing a fluorescent lamp on your head?"

Please don't, Alice!

"...Ω? ǽǽ, œœ... Er, uhhh... Ah, this planet's language is this one."

"Sh-she speaks," says Lilith, shocked to find that the angel can fluently speak the local language.

"Well, I mean, she's got a human-ish head, so I'm sure she can at least talk, Lady Lilith."

"Alice, can you be a little bit more respectful? Do you know who you're addressing?"

Alice doesn't spare the least bit of concern toward the angel, even as the heavenly figure spreads motes of light with her every move.

"It's one of those cosplay creatures, right? The kind that spawns by the dozens at comic conventions in the summer and winter."

"Cosplayers aren't wildflowers that pop up after the rain, Alice! More importantly, treat that person with respect," Lilith barks while taking cover behind me.

"What the hell are you so afraid of anyway? Considering your designs for the Kisaragi combat armor and the racy outfits the Supreme Leaders wear, you're pretty much the same as them."

"Look, just listen to me. Alice, come over here. Please. I'm begging you."

As Lilith pleads with Alice, her metal tentacles emerge from under her lab coat.

…But Alice casually sidesteps and approaches the angel as though driven by curiosity.

"…Hmm. Seems a bit different from the hologram Grimm made the other day."

My partner, completely unfazed by anything and everything, cups one of the angel's boobs.

Apparently, she wanted to see if the angel was tangible, but satisfied with the sensation, she continues to grope away.

As Lilith and Grimm look about ready to faint, I'm treated to the strange sight of a blonde girl fondling a white-haired angel.

I mean, sure, I did something like that to Snow, but my partner's a little too fearless.

The angel, despite being groped, seems unperturbed by Alice's actions and opens her mouth to speak with an unflappable calm.

"…Child of man."

"I'm not a child of man; I'm a child of machines. How much were you paid to be here? Given your looks and acting ability, you'd make more working for me."

Okay, my partner's gutsiness is going way too far.

"Since you're the one who made that android, I'll leave matters to you if a fight breaks out."

"I did create her, but it's your fault she ended up that way. If a fight does break out, I'm running."

As we're busy trying to transfer responsibility in hushed tones, Alice continues groping the angel.

"You seem to misunderstand, child of man. I have come to this doomed world, drawn by a fervent longing..."

"I keep telling you I'm not a child of man, you stupid cosplayer. I'm not interested in role-playing with you. Instead, why don't you tell me how you ended up here?"

What should I do? As her partner, do I have a responsibility to stop Alice?

...The stalwart angel seems to find herself at a loss at Alice's continued handsiness.

"...Child of man, supplicate thyself before me and listen well to my words...o-ow...! For goodness' sake, let go of me!"

"Who's the one who needs to listen? I keep telling you, I'm a child of machines! You want me to rip these tits off?"

Having her breasts relentlessly manhandled, the sedate, collected angel finally raises her voice.

Swatting Alice's hand aside, she rises from the ground.

"I am the Seraph of Mercy and Bonds, El—"

"Why's the lamp on your head floating? You using some rare earth magnet? Also, you keep leaving behind a bunch of shimmering dander every time you flap your wings. You should take responsibility and clean that up."

Alice, could you please shut up already?

...As Elwhatever is interrupted in the middle of her introduction, she retains her cool demeanor but begins quivering with rage.

"I had only come to this doomed world on a whim. However...

if you insist on committing this act of blasphemy upon a servant of the gods, you shall suffer the consequences... Ashes to ashes, dust to dust...let thy soul return to the gods... S-stop it!"

Just as Elwhatever points her finger and begins to say something, Alice wields her vacuum, using the wand to catch one of the angel's wings in the suction.

"Could you knock it off already? Quit making me play along with your and Grimm's idiotic role-playing."

"Stop...! S-stop it! Please stop using that on my wings! It takes over five hours to get them just so!"

With her previous intimidating aura having vanished into thin air, Elwhatever tearfully tries to avoid Alice's vacuum.

"Hey, Grimm, you summoned that angel. Take responsibility already and do something."

"N-no way! Do you understand what that thing just tried to do to Alice? 'Ashes to ashes, dust to dust...let thy soul return to the gods'... It was using an instant-death attack. I have no idea how Alice survived, but I'm NOT getting in the middle of that."

Wait, instant-death attack? That sounds really dangerous.

But I have a fair idea as to why it didn't work on Alice.

It's because she's an android.

"Stop it! Fine, I'll leave! Leave my feathers alone! Please!"

"I'm cleaning your dandruff-covered wings. Least you could do is thank me."

"This is just my divine aura overflowing as particles; it's not dandruff! These are actually blessed items!"

After having various parts of her poked at with a vacuum cleaner, Elwhatever's wings are a mess, with feathers arrayed every which way.

"I come in response to a fervent wish, and this is what I get?! ...You there, the one who summoned me!"

"E-eeep! Y-yesh?!"

With her feathers in disarray, Elwhatever remains floating in the air, pointing an accusatory finger at Grimm.

"Follower of Zenarith, I see that you went through the trouble of summoning me, the Seraph of Mercy and Bonds, only to subject me to this ridicule! If you so desire to be alone, then alone you shall be!"

Elwhatever's eyes shimmer brightly, bringing forth a mysterious aura overflowing with divine fury.

"What? W-wait, no, wait, wait! I don't want that! All I did was summon you! I didn't do anything…!"

As Grimm desperately tries to plead her case…

"Prophet of Zenarith, Grimm Grimoire! Your name will be cursed! From this day forward, you shall only meet men with serious flaws! Enjoy!"

"NOOOOOOOOOOOOOO!"

Hearing the details of Elwhatever's curse, Grimm screams from the depths of her soul.

5

"S-sob…s-sniff…sob…"

After watching Elwhatever curse Grimm and depart for the heavens…

"Could you stop crying already? I mean, c'mon. You already have a tendency to get stuck with weird men. From now on, at least you'll know that everyone you meet has some kind of problem. That's useful, right?"

We've started on our way back to the hideout as Grimm continues sulking in her wheelchair.

"How is that useful?! …Sure, I knew all the men I met had issues… I knew that! But why can't I have a little hope?! All I wanted was to believe that maybe, just maybe, I'd meet *one* who might turn

out to be a wonderful man with no overwhelming flaws. Was it so wrong to want that?! And now...! Now I won't be able to hold out any hope for the men I meet from now on!"

Well, sure, but that's not my fault.

"Now I won't even be able to think *Yeah, I know this guy's got some weird fetish or other potential red flags, but perhaps there's a chance...* There isn't even a smidgen of possibility for that anymore. No matter how handsome they may be, I'll have to worry they might actually be a woman, or however kind they may be, I'll have to worry they're only after me for my money... I won't be able to enjoy so much as a simple give-and-take relationship!"

Grimm's so defeated, she can't even be bothered to move her own wheelchair.

And so, I dutifully wheel around my whiny subordinate.

"I mean, it's sort of your own fault for getting fed up with Alice and summoning all these weirdos. First a demon, then an angel. Aren't you supposed to be the archbishop of the dark god who handles the undead?"

"Don't call Lord Zenarith a dark god!"

After spending some time moaning in her wheelchair, Grimm seems to come to a realization.

"...That's right. There's still one path left for me! Lord Zenarith! Maybe my revered Lord Zenarith is actually super handsome, and no longer being able to take my despair..."

"I'm not one hundred percent on this, but I think your god might actually be a goddess."

"Why are you killing my last glimmer of hope?! Are you that upset by the prospect of me meeting someone, Commander?! Then why don't you take me yourself?!"

I mean, didn't you mention that you were getting chewed out by some woman claiming to be Zenarith when you were dead? Wasn't she yelling at you to stop dying for such stupid reasons?

While I wheel along the despairing Grimm, Lilith is lecturing Alice behind me.

"Listen to me, Alice. You're an android, so I know you don't have it, but people have this thing called instinct. And *that* was a presence that people simply cannot challenge. It's brave to stand up to the powerful, but *that* was on a completely different level."

"Right. Whatever you say, Lady Lilith. Now, I want to do research on the feathers and dandruff I gathered from that cosplayer, so can I go on ahead?"

"No, you may not! Also, stop calling that material 'dandruff.'"

I'm a bit worried that my partner's just gathering really dangerous stuff.

Hell, are we sure feathers from an angel are something that should even exist on this planet…?

"Commander, are you listening? Do you even understand why I'm so upset? It's because you haven't shown the slightest intention of giving me a necklace…"

"Listen, I actually did get one for you. But the Sky King took it from me during Lady Lilith's mission."

I didn't mean anything by those words, but Grimm stops squirming in despair.

"…Really? No doubt you're just getting my hopes up so you can disappointment me again, Commander. I've figured it out, you know. You say the things I want to hear, then blame the Sky King. I know already. I won't be fooled that easily."

Even as she says this, she steals little glances at me. What a pain.

…Huh.

Speaking of pains…

"Hey, Alice, can you give me some of the materials you gathered from the angel?"

"Are you kidding me? Why should I, given how freaked out you were by that cosplay girl? If you want them, you should start address-ing me with some respect."

"I'm not sure how many times I have to repeat myself, but I am your *creator*."

While Alice and Lilith have their routine back-and-forth, I can't shake the feeling that we've been missing someone ever since the Sky King operation...

"Hey, Commander? Could it be that you're actually happy I won't ever meet any decent men from now on? Are you feeling a lit-tle relieved by the fact that there won't be anyone coming after me...? Honestly, I'm happy to know how you feel about me...but we're still not formally engaged, you know, so getting hung up on me is..."

I ignore Grimm the rest of the way back to the hideout.

As my three companions continue fussing, I quicken my pace. Would it kill them to keep the noise down? At this rate, they're gonna wake up the entire neighborhood.

"I mean, what sort of lousy excuse for a Supreme Leader are you, cowering from a cosplayer?"

"Is that any way to speak to your creator?! Alice, I'm running some tests on you when we get back to base!"

I've gotta say, these are some of the most peaceful days I've had since becoming a Combat Agent.

CHAPTER 4

Vs.......

1

Due to Alice's relentless teasing over being terrified of a "cosplayer," Lilith's holed up in her tent.

Three days have passed since I decided to leave that bothersome boss to her own devices.

And today, it's just getting to be evening.

Under the direction of Alice the Ghost Hunter, the hideout is finally complete.

It's a fortress standing a comfortable distance from the Great Woods, its outer walls coated with antilaser paint. Now the savages and their mysterious attacks won't be able to put a scratch on it.

And if the monsters from the woods attack, the barbed-wire fencing surrounding the perimeter will slow them up until the scores of heavy machine guns mounted inside the fortress turn them into Swiss cheese.

"Look at this, Alice. It's our castle. This is where the epic story of Mr. Combat Agent Six and his useless subordinates will begin."

"And just who are you including among those useless subordinates? I'm not your subordinate; I'm your partner. So let's change the story title to *The Rise of Six, Alice, and Co.*"

While we're looking over the wastelands and woods from the rooftop of the giant fortress, a voice calls over from behind us.

"...Hey, um, I'm nowhere to be found among any of those titles..."

After spending the last few days shut up in her tent talking to the orange crawfish, Lilith finally emerges just in time for our move-in day.

"The hideout's done, Lady Lilith, so you'll be able to go home in a month or so."

Lilith purses her lips in a pout at my ironclad logic.

"So you're just going to leave me out of it, Six? You went to the trouble of specifically asking for me to come here. Aren't there other things you could be saying? Something like how you'll be lonely without me here, or suggesting I stay a little bit longer. There are so many nicer things you could say..."

I do my best to just let my bothersome boss's bothersome complaints go in one ear and out the other, when Alice lightly tugs at Lilith's lab coat.

"On that note, Lady Lilith, it looks like you'll be able to go home in less than a month. It's the second time we've conducted portal stabilization. With my superior skills, I've managed to shorten the time to two weeks. You're welcome to praise me, of course."

The emotions behind the look Lilith gives Alice are surprisingly hard to identify.

"I—I see. Well done, Alice. But choosing now, of all times, to mention that feels intentionally cruel on your part..."

Lilith looks totally defeated, perhaps because she hasn't had a real win since she got here.

"Oh, it's not like I'm trying to get rid of you because you're worth even less than the food you're consuming. It's not like I want you to leave because I'm sick of your picky orders for dinner."

"Alice, are you sure you're not in a rebellious phase?! I don't remember equipping you with the ability to mouth off to your creator! I am your *god*, remember?! Your loving parent! Would it kill you to be a little nicer to me?!"

Lilith tearfully pleads with Alice. I guess all the disrespect is really wearing her down.

"Lady Lilith, let's focus on something more important. How are we going to annihilate our competition? I mean, that's honestly the reason I wanted you here."

Yes, my true goal in requesting Lilith was to use her overpowered Supreme Leader abilities to blow away the competition.

Now that the hideout is complete and we have a foothold for conquering the planet, our next highest priority is to take out our competitor, the Demon Lord's Army, in order to nip any potential threats in the bud.

Unfortunately, Lilith averts her gaze at that comment, looking a bit uncomfortable.

"...Demon Lord's Army, Demon Lord's Army... Reading the reports, it seemed like they'd be easy enough to take out, but...what are they really like? Let's remember that the giant lizard, the giant sparrow, and the giant slime weren't in any of the reports I got."

Lilith's understandably cautious, seeing as she's been tossed up against foe after imposing foe ever since she arrived.

"There are a few that are kind of strong, but I'm sure they're no match for you, Lady Lilith."

"Yeah. The most they have is a giant robot that can damage a Destroyer and a handful of leaders that are mutant-class in terms of abilities. I'm sure Lady Lilith would make quick work of them."

As Alice and I try to reassure her, Lilith starts fidgeting.

"...You know my actual role is to serve as the brains and not the brawn, right? There's the one-in-ten-thousand chance that something will go wrong, so maybe I should go back to Earth and send Belial in my stead… I mean, think about it. With my method of fighting, I would burn through a massive amount of Evil Points in no time at all. It would be a great loss for Kisaragi if I ran out of points and lost most of my firepower."

Our words fall on deaf ears, and our useless boss starts fishing for excuses.

I guess being faced with the ultimate authority of the angel was too much for our timid little science geek.

"What's going on? Did the angel freak you out that badly?"

"I c-can't help that! My instincts were screaming *you'll never win against that thing* the whole time! In fact, the eviler you are, the more afraid you would be of a holy being like that. With the atrocities I've committed, I couldn't hope for redemption even if I spent the rest of my life doing good deeds."

…I'm in the same boat, actually.

Noticing that I've grown silent next to Lilith, my partner, who absolutely loathes all things supernatural, suddenly snaps.

"You're all just a bunch of cowards. Wave the banner of evil proudly! Give God the middle finger! Lady Lilith, how the hell can you call yourself *my* creator, huh? Huh?!"

"No, the question is more why you, as one of my creations, are so hostile to the notion of gods. I'm really growing worried about you… I'm scared you're going to do something terrible the moment I take my eyes off you…"

Alice looks fed up, but in all honesty, I'm afraid of supernatural stuff like ghosts and angels, too.

The reason we villains can commit to our villainy is because we don't believe in an afterlife.

I'm not as bad as Lilith, but I've done a lot of blasphemous stuff, like stealing money from offering boxes at shrines or peeing on the entrance gates. I've pretty much secured myself a one-way ticket to hell.

"…Tch, what am I going to do with this wimp of a parent? Yo, Six, we'll do something about the Demon Lord's Army on our own. I mean, now that we've got this hideout, it's just a matter of time."

"Huh?"

Having my hopes for total annihilation of the enemy at the hands of a Supreme Leader utterly dashed, I can't hold back a surprised gasp.

Lilith, on the other hand, lets out a sigh of relief.

"…As for you, Lady Lilith, now that we have no idea why you bothered coming here, the least you can do is go survey those weird ruins."

"Huh?"

Fresh beads of sweat appear on Lilith's brow.

Alice's harsher-than-expected critique has paralyzed her with shock.

Alice continues, having caught the sympathetic glance I offered the frozen Lilith.

"Not to spoil your schadenfreude, Six, but you're going with her."

"Huh?"

2

Even on this alien planet, the sun still sets.

Grasping the fencing on the hideout rooftop and gazing out over the wastelands as the sun sets over the horizon, Lilith speaks in a solemn murmur.

"Alice, can you get me some coffee? No need for sugar. Just hot and black."

"Huh? Get it yourself. Who the hell do you think you are?"

……

"Hold up, Alice! Your attitude's getting even worse!"

"I'm just taking after my creator."

"There's no way that's true! Sure, I can be passive-aggressive, but I don't throw barbs like that! Can you please just get me some coffee?! Please just fulfill a simple request from your parent, for once!"

At Lilith's pained shriek, Alice twists her face into an irritated grimace despite supposedly being an android and ploddingly goes off to make some coffee.

After spending a few moments getting her ragged breathing under control, Lilith looks up as though she's regained a measure of composure.

"…Sorry about that, Six. I didn't mean for you to see that embarrassing display."

"Wait, how was that any different from usual?"

Seems she wants to play this out as a serious scene, but she's just not the boss for this sort of thing.

Reading the mood, I keep any further comments to myself and also turn my gaze to the setting sun.

"Ever since I got to this planet, nothing has gone right."

Lilith seems to be muttering half to herself and half to me.

Ordinarily, the self-proclaimed genius is pride made manifest, but looking out over the woods and wastelands spreading out below, she's having one of her rare moments of weakness.

"What's wrong, Lady Lilith? Usually, you don't care what anyone says to you. You'll just pick your nose as their words go in one ear and out the other. This isn't like you."

"I've been wondering this for a while, but I want to know what you Combat Agents really think of me… Actually, no, never mind. Considering my usual behavior, it's probably best not to listen to that. There are times when even I get hurt, you know."

At least she has enough self-awareness to know she probably won't like what she hears.

"I came to this planet, fully expecting to solve all its problems, and yet…everything I try to do here seems to go wrong. Based on my original plans, I should be preparing to burn the competition's castle to the ground and drag Six back to Earth…"

"You know I'm not going home anytime soon, right? My Evil Points are still in the red. If I go back now, I'm gonna get snatched up by the punishment squad."

…At that, Lilith looks at me quizzically.

"…Huh, Alice hasn't told you yet? I was going to help you pay off your Evil Point debt."

……

"Huh? Seriously, Lady Lilith? Wait, I didn't even know you could trade Evil Points."

As I lean forward at that piece of news, Lilith breaks out in a malicious smile.

"What are you talking about? Obviously, you can't trade Evil Points. I'm going to help you pay off your debt by helping you commit an act of villainy big enough that you'll be able to come home."

…Oh great, another harebrained scheme.

My exasperation must have shown, because Lilith lets out a dry chuckle and shrugs.

"I know what you're thinking: that you're not capable of doing something that evil. But remember, Six, even as you're playing around here, you've got people on Earth eagerly awaiting your return… Yes. Friends who care much more about your well-being than any number of cross-dressing Chimeras, gold-digging knights, and hot-mess cultists ever could."

Lilith's probably talking about my two other bosses.

My beloved bosses, who've dragged me along over the years since Kisaragi's founding, despite the fact that I'm not all that powerful. They've stuck with me through all of it and refused to abandon me.

I mean, in all honesty, I really do just want to go back to Earth.

Even with the hideout's completion, this is hardly an ideal quality of life.

While I'm stuck on this rock, I need to spend Evil Points just to buy a porn mag, and there's no TV or manga here.

If I go back to Earth, there won't be women devouring orc meat in front of me, and I won't have to be overly cautious every time I order skewered meat off the street.

But...

"I appreciate the thought, but who would take over for me? Tiger Man loves fighting on the front lines, while the other Combat Agents are all idiots."

"I mean, considering that you, the dumbest of all the Combat Agents, have lasted this long, I'm sure the next person will be fine. Besides, we'll be leaving Alice on this world. So long as she's around, it doesn't matter who takes over for you."

...Wait, what?

"Seriously? But if Alice stays here, who'll take care of me? I need her to do things like keep track of my allowance."

"Y-you know, you should be doing that sort of thing on your own. You're a grown man... Still, considering how much you two bickered when we first sent you out here, you seem to have gotten pretty close."

With that, she flashes a teasing smile...

"Yeah...does Alice even know about this?"

"Of course. She raised quite a fuss when I told her I'd be dragging you home. It doesn't seem like she's fully come to terms with it yet."

Hearing those words, I feel a sense of relief that Alice doesn't consider me unnecessary and isn't eager to send me back.

Well, in that case.

"I'm sorry. I appreciate the thought, but I'd like to stay on this planet a bit longer."

"No."

......

"Are the Heroes back on Earth really becoming that much of a problem? Is it really gonna take Kisaragi's ace in the hole, yours truly, to come save the day?"

"I honestly have no idea what's going on in that head of yours. I—I mean, sure, we need as many Combat Agents as we can get our hands on, but...there's a different reason for recalling you."

Lilith turns to me and stares intently into my eyes.

"...Combat Agent Six, you've gotten weaker since you've come here, haven't you? You've gotten so used to this easy life that you've forgotten you're an operative for an evil organization, haven't you?"

I feel like Lilith's peering straight into my soul, and I can't look away.

It's then that I remember something Alice said when we first got here.

"It's probably less that the Supreme Leaders are pinching pennies and more the fact that they want you to commit acts of villainy. Start small, gradually work up to bigger acts of evil, and end up a proper Supreme Leader candidate," or something like that.

...Dammit.

"...Why are you looking at me like that, Lady Lilith? You want me to smooch you that badly?"

"...Ha, like you'd have the stones... No, no, I'm sorry. I lied. You look like you really might do it! I forgot that, for things like this, you actually do follow through on threats. I'm sorry! Forgive me!"

Seeing my serious expression, Lilith lets loose a stream of apologies.

"...Still, Six, you really have gotten weaker since you've been here... No, that's not quite right. It's not that you're weaker. You've just gone soft..."

......

"What are you going on about, Lady Lilith? You've seen how

harsh this planet's environment is. I mean, you're one to talk, considering you freaked out over an angel and are so worried about a Demon Lord that you're trying to run home to avoid fighting him!"

"Sh-shut up! There's nothing wrong with me doing that, since I'm the brainy sort! But you're a Combat Agent. Your only value is in your combat ability!"

Lilith smacks the fence in irritation, then reaches for my head.

"I'll just go ahead and say it. Everyone's waiting for you to come back to Earth. To see you come back stronger after surviving this rough environment. But what the hell is with your recent reports? All those soft, sweet ramblings!"

Lilith grabs my head and begins roughly tussling my hair, letting out all the frustration that's built up during our time apart.

"What the hell are you doing, making a harem out on this nothing planet? How could you let some random new floozies control you like that? I come here thinking you're working hard, and instead, I find you staring up the skirt of a cross-dressing Chimera, getting uncomfortably close with Boobzilla, and then to top it all off, you're engaged! We told you to investigate the planet and then conquer it! Never once did we mention anything about conquering women instead!"

"Lady Lilith, I find your accusation of me being close to Boobzilla insulting."

I interjected because I couldn't let that point go uncontested, but Lilith's anger shows no signs of subsiding.

"Shut up! It's time for you to listen to me! …We were all hoping that if we tossed you into a harsh environment, you'd go from still being a half-decent person deep down to a proper villain…"

My useless boss keeps hold of the fence with one hand, standing on tiptoe to shove my head with the other.

"The hell are you doing, flirting with random women while everyone's busy fighting on Earth?! We've known you longer than they have, so stop talking like you plan to take up permanent residence on this planet! You're *our* flunky, not theirs!"

......

What am I supposed to do this with annoying *tsundere* boss?

After sending me out, the moment I start settling in here, they demand I come back.

It's not like they're gonna pamper me when I get back to Earth.

What a pain.

These people are such a handful...

But...

"I'm sorry, Lady Lilith. It's true; I've enjoyed my time on this planet. But let me at least say this..."

Just as I'm about to say something important to Lilith, standing there on the verge of tears...

"Hey, you, Lady Horndog. How dare you send me off to fetch you coffee while you're here flirting!"

""Wait, this isn't what it looks like!""

Despite having nothing to hide, Lilith and I respond in unison.

3

After Lilith flees back to her room, Alice and I stand on the rooftop, looking up at a sky filled with stars.

With a Supreme Leader coming over here, I knew my days on this rock were limited, but...

"It's all moving so quickly..."

"What's with the long face? Got something on your mind?"

Oh, right, she's staying behind.

I wonder what'll happen to this planet once I go home, leaving Alice bereft of her partner and conscience.

"Hey, Alice, what do you think of your mission on this planet anyway? Are you really planning to take over the place?"

"Well, of course. You do recall we were sent here to secure enough land for humanity's survival, right? Failure means the end of humanity."

...Oh yeah. I'd forgotten just how important our mission is.

It's something I learned only recently, but the various problems facing the Earth are a lot more serious than most people are led to believe.

The general public thinks we still have a couple hundred years of fossil-fuel reserves left, but the reality is we're gonna run out in a few decades.

The issue of feeding the growing population will to lead to war if things stay the way they are.

As for pollution, things are a lot worse than people are led to believe, and we might very well be past the point of no return.

According to Lilith the scientist, the problems are so bad that the only real solution is for humanity to go extinct...

If word gets out, there's going to be mass panic and chaos in the streets. There's nothing quite like having no hope for the future to make people do stupid things.

I guess it's like Snow not knowing about the Mud King slumbering beneath this very kingdom.

Frankly, I would've been better off not knowing about that.

Even if the world's countries try to come together for the sake of humanity's future, they won't be able to put aside their old grudges and petty interests, and the situation's too dire to let them fight it out. It's cruel irony that the only solution is for an evil organization like us to force everyone to do what's best.

"...Still, it's not like things will get worse for the locals of this planet. From my investigations, the amount of settled land on this world is small. Only about three percent of the globe is populated. My guess is that, at this rate, both humans and demons are doomed to extinction."

While I'm waxing sentimental, the android chimes in with a reality check.

"...Dammit! No hope for either world, huh? We find a pretty, new planet, only to discover that everyone's still in a hell of a fix. At this rate, I'm never gonna get to live out my days in decadence."

I lie down on the hard, concrete roof, whining as I gaze up at the sky.

Alice lies down to join me and stares up at the sky herself.

"Yeah, on this planet, a bunch of tiny kingdoms are clinging to life on a handful of livable areas. Everyone's busy fighting monsters and natural disasters. The war against the Demon Lord's Army is really the least of their worries. It'd be easier if we could just find an undeveloped world with no dangerous life-forms, but..."

We come all the way to an alien planet brimming with fantastic possibilities, and yet the harsh grip of reality won't let go.

From up here on the roof, the night sky looks sparklingly clear, perhaps due to the lack of pollution.

As I drink in the unfamiliar constellations hovering overhead, I fully realize I'm not on Earth anymore.

Keeping my gaze on the sky, I ask Alice:

"...Hey, Alice, you've heard from Lady Lilith, right? I'm going back to Earth with her once the survey on the ruins is done."

"Yep, I've known about that for ages. Once you leave, things are gonna get busy around here."

...Huh?

"Aw, Alice, are you saying you're gonna end up with a lot more work once you no longer have my superior abilities to support you? First Lady Lilith, now you. You two oughta just say how you really feel more often."

"No, that's not it. I'll just have a lot more freedom when I'm not stuck babysitting you anymore. The conquest of this planet's going to take a great leap forward, so I'll have a lot to do."

Despite the ideal setting—gazing up at a beautiful night sky on an alien world—this snarky android is busy insulting me.

I guess she can't help it; she's just a machine.

She can't understand her partner getting sentimental at the idea of parting.

"Oh yeah? That's rich coming from you, Alice. I remember you talking about how much of a meathead I was when we first met. And now what? I'm being recalled to Earth because I'm priceless!"

Despite my gloating, Alice shows no annoyance or regret that we'll soon go our separate ways.

"...Y-yeah? That's nice. Sure, you're plenty useful. Take care of yourself when you get home... Listen up, okay? When you get back to Earth, Lady Belial's probably going to order you to go support her. Say that you got food poisoning from something you ate on this planet and shirk those orders for as long as you can."

....

"Huh, wait just a minute. I'm gonna get sent somewhere after I return to Earth? Where's Lady Belial fighting right now? Okay, you convinced me; I'm staying."

I find myself losing my nerve at Alice's warning.

"...No. If my guess is off, you'll be on easy street at headquarters."

Alice speaks without meeting my eyes, but now I'm desperate for confirmation.

"I've yet to see your guesses not pan out! Goddammit, how did I end up in this situation anyway?! This is all Lady Lilith's fault! She's so damn useless. I'm gonna sneak her some pork and say, *Wow, I didn't know you liked orc meat!*"

"Count me in when you do that. Lady Lilith pretends to be a gourmand, but she doesn't know the first thing about fine dining. That nouveau riche boss will happily devour orc meat if you tell her it's foie gras."

I'm pretty sure she'd be able to tell the difference between foie gras and orc meat, but given the weird gaps in Lilith's knowledge, I find it more than plausible.

"That good-for-nothing boss always asks too much of us. Every week, she sends me off to buy her weekly manga magazines when they release, even if it's on my day off."

"It's completely unacceptable that she sends her subordinates to run her little errands. She made me fetch coffee. The nerve. That's the sort of job for Edo-era tea-pouring dolls, not advanced androids!"

"Yeah, totally! Where does she get off? In fact, she once sent me to—"

Under a sky dotted with stars that bear no resemblance to those looking down on Earth...

...Alice and I while away the hours until the light of the rising sun erases the flickering pinholes in the heavens...just griping about our useless boss.

4

The next day.

"I'm not entirely sure it's safe to go with just myself and the useless Lady Lilith, so I brought along some help."

"I'm the hired help, Patrasche."

"Are you mocking me?!"

I introduce Patrasche to Lilith at the hideout's front gate and promptly get yelled at.

"Why are you so angry, Lady Lilith? This one's the most competent out of my various troops."

"My signature move is an arm lock from a mounted position after a tackle."

After her introduction, Patrasche strikes a fighting pose.

"No, that's not what I'm talking about! Who is this mutant fursuit girl?"

Patrasche, aka Rose, really seems to like her fursuit, so she's been living as Patrasche even after the Undead Festival.

"There's a deep reason for this. See, she usually spends her days as an old man's pet."

"A-an old man's pet?! What the hell does that mean?! Based on the voice, that's a young girl in there, isn't there?"

Kisaragi has a zero-tolerance policy when it comes to sex crimes against children.

Seems Lilith has jumped to the wrong conclusion and looks extremely angry.

"No, you've got the wrong idea, Lady Lilith. She's a growing girl and eats a lot, so we're fooling the old man and having him feed her."

"I even get dessert."

"I can't understand what the heck you're trying to say! Despite having one of the greatest minds in human history, I can't make heads or tails of what you're talking about! This planet really is just full of nonsense!"

Evidently, this is all too much for Lilith to process, and she's cradling her head, letting out a cry of despair.

I mean, sure, we're scamming the old man, but it's a harmless white lie that leaves everyone happy. No harm, no foul.

"She may look kind of ridiculous, but when it comes to combat, she can give me a run for my money."

"I'm ready to go, ma'am! I'm also ready to gnaw on the boss as needed!"

Ignoring Rose, Lilith turns her back on us.

"I'm not going to try to make sense of this anymore! Let's head to the ruins!"

Rose and I follow Lilith as she starts toward the woods.

"Oh, as an aside—in an emergency, she's got a breath attack."

"Fire breath, to be specific."

"Wait, I can't just ignore that! What's that all about? Just who are you, Patrasche?!"

I'm giving Rose the rundown on Lady Lilith as we make our way to the ruins.

"So Lady Lilith is the one responsible for sending me to this planet. That's why I planned to get a little revenge by fooling her into coming here as well, but she's been totally useless ever since she arrived."

Once this mission's over, both Lilith and I are heading back to Earth.

Given Lilith's usual shyness and her introvert's tendency to misjudge how close she is to people, it looks like she's decided not to make friends with Rose, seeing as she'll probably have to leave too soon afterward.

* * *

"There are spots here and there that I don't quite understand, but essentially, without Lady Lilith's orders, Boss wouldn't have come to this kingdom, right?"

Despite being inside a cumbersome animal suit, Rose cuts us a path through the obnoxiously deep woods.

...I don't know if it's because she's a highly adaptable Chimera, but I'm impressed. How is she able to waltz through these woods like that?

"Yeah, I guess that's true. You know, I really thought I was done for, given that she teleported me way up into the air. I was so angry that I swore if I ever got back to Earth, I'd grope Lady Lilith until she cried."

At my last sentence, Lilith, who's been keeping her distance, shudders.

The Supreme Leader responsible for tricking me into coming to this place hurriedly begins making excuses.

"S-Six, wait just a moment. There was a good reason for that. The first teleportation always has a margin of error. If you wound up inside the planet or deep under the sea, you'd have no chance of survival. And when it comes to teleporting you onto the surface, it's impossible to do so near the ground. But if we sent you up into the sky, it'd be at a height from which you could survive a fall. Neither you nor Alice would fall fast enough to burn up in the stratosphere."

......Say whaaaaaaaaaaaaaaaaaaaaaaaat?!

"Wait, what'd you just say? You teleported us into the stratosphere on purpose?! If you'd sent me a little higher, I would've been in space, dammit!"

Lilith trembles as I approach but continues speaking.

"Y-you still would've survived that! You Combat Agents have enough modifications to survive around three minutes even in deep space! Even if you'd ended up there, I figured the planet's gravity would catch you in time. B-besides, it worked out in the end, so I was right!"

This damn brat is really trying to turn this on me now!

Despite her excuses, this boss from hell seems to realize she's at a disadvantage, as she backs away, eyeing me warily.

"You really think I'm just gonna let you make me out to be the unreasonable one here?! Listen, short stack, I'm definitely groping you till you cry!"

"Did you just call your boss a short stack?! I'm going to tell Astaroth about this at the Supreme Leader meeting and have her yell at you… W-wait, Six! Okay, why don't we talk?! What do you want? Do you want me to set something up for you?"

The boss from hell, well aware she's getting nowhere, begins trying to negotiate as I stomp closer.

"As a Supreme Leader, I have a fair bit of influence, you know… Stop! Don't come any closer! Y-you sure about this?! You wanna fight?! You know I'll kick your ass, right?!"

Lilith, with a pleading expression, opens her lab coat so she can quickly deploy her tentacles in a show of intimidation, but at that moment…

…a soft chuckling emerges from the fursuit, which looks completely out of place in the middle of the woods.

While I can't see her expression because of the getup, Rose is quaking with laughter.

"Ah-ha-ha-ha… You know, Lady Lilith and Boss, you two are less like supervisor and subordinate and more like friends!"

"Hold on there, Mutant Fursuit Girl, this useless Combat Agent is more like a failure of a younger brother than a friend. Do you have any idea how much trouble this man causes me…?"

"Say what?! Why am I, your literal senior, the younger brother, you useless boss?! I constantly get stuck with missions that are basically putting out your brush fires! I'm the one being screwed by you!"

As the two of us exchange close-range insults, Rose keeps laughing.

"I feel like I'm watching a fight between you and Snow, Boss. I mean, I have to thank you, Lady Lilith! If you'd sent someone else instead of the boss here…it's possible we'd have been monster food by now!"

......

Rose drops a pretty heavy endorsement despite her cheery demeanor, and the two of us feel our hostility melt away as we exchange glances.

"Hey, Six, this fursuit girl… In contrast to her dumb appearance, she's saying some pretty deep stuff."

"Well, she's got a bit of a history herself. The reason she's dressed like this is because she's pretending to be the dead pet of an old man who doesn't have much time left."

Hearing this, Lilith turns to Rose, whom she'd been avoiding until now.

"…Six, does that mean Patrasche might be the most normal of your subordinates?"

"Well, for one thing, when she's hungry, she has no problem eating orc meat. Hell, she even tried to devour me once… Still, she's our squad's conscience."

......

"Wait, I just heard something I can't ignore. When you say she tried to 'devour you,' did you mean that in a pervy way?"

"Nope, I meant it in the food way. She literally tried to eat me."

5

Although Lilith initially backed far away from Rose, they eventually got past the misunderstanding, and now they're getting along pretty well.

"—Which is when I told them: We're part of the forces of darkness, wrapping the night around us and sleeping in death's cradle. Leave now, or you'll never see the dawn to this night… Cool, right?"

"That's impressive, Lady Lilith! That's the sort of line my grandpa used to say!"

Lilith has taken a shine to Rose, who has a tendency to make various painfully awkward and melodramatic statements.

Maybe it's understandable. I mean, she does call herself Lilith the Black with a straight face.

She's so cringey that she makes Rose, who was thoroughly infected by her grandfather's bullshit, look normal in comparison.

"My grandpa would often say that the foolish dregs of humanity should just be destroyed by our hand."

"Patrasche, your grandpa doesn't feel like a stranger to me. I used to say similar things when I was a kid."

It's only been a few hours, but it seems they've found common ground. My grandiose boss and delusional subordinate are getting along fabulously.

"Yeah, I can't think of you as a stranger, either, Lady Lilith. Your white clothes, your way of speaking—it all reminds me of my grandpa."

I suppose when I think about it, Lilith and Rose are of a similar age, and neither of them really fit in with the world around them. No doubt they've got a lot in common.

Just then, as though having an epiphany, Lilith goes from cheerful to pensive.

"…Your grandpa wore a lab coat like mine? Meaning he was a scientist on this planet…?"

"I don't know what a scientist is, but he often used to say he was going to make the greatest life-form there ever was, and then he'd cackle in that odd way of his."

The description makes Lilith glance away for some reason.

…Oh yeah, that reminds me. She would often cackle in the operating room, saying something about creating the ultimate mutant.

According to Lilith, it's a sort of ritual before rolling the dice on the mutant lockbox.

From the perspective of the mutant getting modified, it's a hell of a thing to learn that whatever happens comes down to luck.

It's things like this that doom her to perennial unpopularity in the polls.

"Well, unlike the other three lackeys, you're pretty sharp. Oh, look at this, Patrasche. There's a mysterious mushroom growing on the crook of this tree. I've seen them sprout near the roots and rotted trunks plenty of times, but... Hey, wait! Patrasche, stop!"

"They're crunchy and pretty tasty. Would you like some, Lady Lilith?"

No sooner has Lilith pointed out mushrooms growing on the crook of a tree than Rose snatches a handful and begins eating them.

"P-Patrasche, in the wild, you need to be particularly careful with mushrooms. It's risky to just randomly toss them into your mouth... and you're eating those raw..."

Lilith is a bit repulsed as Rose pulls the raw fungi under her mask, crunching into them, and the little scientist does her best to explain the danger.

"I understand, Lady Lilith. I'll make sure to cook them from now on! Oh, there's some pretty mushrooms here, too. I'll take them home and roast them before eating them."

"You're not getting it! You missed my point entirely, Patrasche! Don't eat mushrooms you've never seen before! Especially not ones that are rainbow colored! That's the mushroom's way of saying it's super poisonous!"

Rose, evidently having acquired a taste for poisonous mushrooms, begins gathering more as Lilith frantically tries to stop her.

"I won't tell you not to eat them, but at least wait until I test them."

"I understand, Lady Lilith. Let's make a hot pot out of them once you've finished your tests. Orc meat's been really cheap lately."

Having taken a tour of the farms recently, Lilith's expression freezes at the mention of orc meat.

"Um, are you really that hungry, Patrasche? Six, teach this girl some survival skills. Mushrooms are a big no-no. If you're hungry and facing starvation, then bugs are the best source of nourishment. They look unappetizing, but they've got plenty of nutrients, and most are poison-free."

"Lady Lilith, bugs are the one thing I'd like to avoid eating."

"Uh, Lady Lilith, I can't eat bugs, either."

Our quick responses prompt Lilith to look at us like particularly dim children.

"What sort of miserable excuses for Kisaragi Combat Agents are you two? You're happy to eat orcs capable of human speech, but you're afraid of eating bugs?"

Lilith shrugs her shoulders in exasperation.

"Oh, hey, there's a purple cricket over there, Rose. It's croaking like a frog. Grab it for Lady Lilith's lunch."

"Leave it to me, Lady Lilith! I'll go grab it!"

"Okay, okay, I was wrong! A croaking cricket is a bit beyond even my ability to eat! I'm sorry! Please forgive me!"

6

Six hours after departing the hideout.

We've finally arrived at the ruins, which are actually just a stone's throw from our base.

"We're finally here, Patrasche. Even if you see something moving, don't put it into your mouth, okay?"

"I'd appreciate it if you don't go wandering off every time something catches your eye, Lady Lilith. These woods are full of dangerous critters."

The main reason it's taken us so long to get here is these two:

Rose, who tries to down anything that looks remotely edible, and Lilith, who can't resist pocketing anything remotely peculiar.

Because these two have taken their sweet time, the sun's already dipping under the horizon.

"What are we gonna do now, Lady Lilith? The plan was to wander over, go inside, and do a little surveying, but it'll be a chore getting back to the hideout at this time of day."

I warily look around and provide a word of warning to Lilith and Rose, who are sitting at the entrance to the ruins, seemingly worn out from all their earlier excitement.

"It'd be a hassle to go home now and come back later. Why don't we just stay for the night and survey the ruins in the morning? With me here, we won't have to worry about the monsters, at least."

Lilith has a smile on her face, but this is the sort of situation where it's dangerous to count on this boss.

"Why don't we take a quick look around inside first, just in case? Right now, the only future I'm imagining is you letting your guard down and throwing a tantrum after some dangerous creature attacks you."

"...I hate it when you say stuff like that. You have a weird way of predicting these things... I wanted to rest, but fine, let's take care of one last errand, Patrasche."

"Understood, Lady Lilith. Leave surveying these ruins to me. My memories of Grandpa include playing in a place like this!"

Rose has occasionally said odd things like this while warming up to Lilith. Soon, we set foot inside the ruins the giant lizard had been guarding just the other day.

For some reason, the interior is well lit, but thanks to the depth charge Lilith used when fighting the giant lizard, it's also a disaster zone.

"...I heard a giant lizard was guarding this place, but it looks like it didn't do its job very well."

Rose makes her oblivious comment, and Lilith shoots me a glance, warning me to stay quiet.

"Oh, the reason things are a mess in here is because of a weapon Lady Lilith used. The lizard was actually doing a good job."

"Hey! Traitor!"

Unlike last time when we only glanced inside, Lilith is closely examining the ruins, and something seems to have taken her aback.

"...Hey, Six, didn't you say you searched through another ruin? Were the walls there made of the same material?"

Lilith's expression is, for once, that of a researcher. She squints as she runs her hands along the walls.

"Do you really think I'd remember something like that? ...Oh, but Snow was trying to carve out pieces of the walls and the wreckage to take home. She was going on about how, since we didn't find any treasure, at the very least, she was gonna sell the scrap."

"I—I see. You know, if she's willing to go that far, I'm actually kind of impressed at Snow's dedication to money. Greed is one thing, but that's a higher level of commitment than I was expecting. She definitely feels like the sort who'd stop at nothing to get cash."

That's true. She's the sort who'd sell her body if she could still ride a unicorn after.

...Lilith tilts her head in confusion as she feels the wall.

"Hmm...the numbers just don't add up..."

Rose and I exchange glances at this.

"What is it, Lady Lilith? As long as it's within two digits, I won't screw up adding or subtracting. Since I'm your assistant today, let me know if there's anything I can do to help."

"And I can count up to twenty-one using my fingers, toes, and tail."

"Right. I appreciate the thought. Thank you. But let me be absolutely clear that while we're on assignment, you two need to stick with someone else who can handle the thinking."

After making that weird comment, Lilith resumes muttering to herself.

"The tank that was discarded in the Grace Kingdom had clearly deteriorated from age. But the walls of these ruins show no signs of rust or wear, even though they're clearly metal. If they have this sort of technology, why not use it on a tank? Sure, there's the possibility this metal is too heavy or otherwise unsuited for the entire frame, but...even then, they'd at least coat the surface with it..."

As Lilith loses herself in her thoughts...

"Hey, Rose, looks like this is gonna take a while, so let's play some tic-tac-toe. It's a game where the one who lines up five *O*'s or *X*'s wins. Let's say we're betting on tonight's dinner."

"Yes, I accept! I love that we're betting food instead of money."

...Oh!

"Just so we're clear, it's for ONE meal, okay? And it's not all-you-can-eat. If I win, it's not like I'll eat that much, but you always randomly eat enough for ten people!"

"Boss, you're the boss, so don't be so stingy. I think generous bosses are the coolest bosses!"

"...Savages who use mysterious energy weapons, a robotic cannon disguised to look like a giant lizard—why do they try to hide traces of advanced technology on this planet? On the other hand, they just leave cheap combat vehicles out in the open. It's almost like they're intentionally placed there as a distraction..."

Thirty minutes later.

Having spent the entire time deep in thought, Lilith looks up as though she's come to a realization.

"Combat Agent Six! There's an important question I need to ask you. In the other ruins you checked, were there any human remains?!

The place where you said the giant robot was stored—was the robot the only thing you found?!"

"Like I keep telling you, child of morons, learn the rules! You can only draw once during your turn, and you can't erase and move your X on another turn!"

"Then how about having my X and Boss's O switch places? Otherwise, this isn't fair! It feels like you have the advantage just by going first, Boss!"

"Fine, we can start over with you going first! I mean, it's like you've never played games before!"

Lilith's brow twitches as she sees us arguing over our tic-tac-toe game.

"What are you two doing in the middle of an important mission?! If you want to play a game, I'll buy you Othello, and you can play to your heart's content *after* we're done."

"I'll take that Othello, but we've gotta finish this tic-tac-toe game first. She just won't learn the rules."

"Grandpa used to say that if humans are creatures that live within the rules, then you, a creature made to destroy humanity, need not follow rules."

Oh, the fact that dinner's on the line is causing her to completely abandon any semblance of restraint.

"Quoting your grandpa whenever it's convenient, huh? There's no way he said that!"

"H-he probably said it! I mean, it's the sort of thing he'd say!"

"I just made a huge discovery. Would you two pipe down a bit? If you keep arguing, you'll get the tentacles!"

After yelling at us, Lilith resumes scrutinizing the ruins.

"...Yeah, that's gotta be it! This place has been abandoned a long time, but the lights still work. And they're electric..."

Despite being a bit turned off by Lilith's enthusiasm, I glance at the lights.

"The glass balls are floating. What is this? There a fairy inside or something?"

"No! Well, I don't know what those fairy creatures are, either, but...this appears to be using ambient electrical fields for power. And it floats because it's either using a material that negates gravity or employing some sort of antigravity technology."

I have no idea what Lilith is talking about, but I nod seriously.

"So it's lit with mystery power and floats using mystery power, right?"

"Not even close!"

I don't understand this complex stuff, but I do notice something.

"Why even go to this trouble? Why not just plug it into an outlet? In the other ruins, the lighting was embedded in the walls."

"That's exactly it! There must be some reason for this. For example...Patrasche, are there a lot of earthquakes around these parts?"

"Huh? Earth...quakes? I've heard they used to happen pretty frequently, but they stopped over the past few decades. Apparently, it was after the Sand King left the area."

Lilith nods as if the pieces are starting to click into place.

She seems to be looking at something far off in the distance, as though she's achieved some sort of enlightenment.

"The Sand King is the giant mole that was in the reports, right? So why did the mole leave the Great Woods, where food was abundant? Could it be there was a monster that actually posed a threat to it? ...For example, the giant lizard I defeated? Ah-ha-ha-ha-ha-ha-ha! ...Six, there are so many things you can learn from just one floating light source. Do you understand the situation?"

Lilith's eyes go from staring into the distance to slowly losing interest. She ends up asking a question almost disinterestedly...

"No, not at all."

"I don't understand it at all, either!"

"Fine. Never mind, then. It's my fault for asking you two in the first place. Alice! Aliiiice! Dammit. No Alice when I actually need to talk to her! What to do, what to do? Guess we cut the survey short and temporarily withdraw all our Combat Agents back to Earth…"

Lilith begins talking to herself again, and just as I completely lose track of what she's saying…

…I hear a deep, rumbling cry coming from the depths of the ruins.

"……Six, I'm going back to the hideout. Go have a look around the lower levels."

"No way. This has gotta be one of those times when the person who checks winds up dead."

I try to assess the current situation based on Lilith's behavior.

This is a scenario that shows up in manga and stuff where, after a terrible secret is uncovered, the true villain arrives to silence the hapless discoverer.

Likely reaching the same conclusion I have, Lilith begins looking around nervously.

"Hey, Six, why don't we head back to Earth? I feel like this planet's got too many potential problems. Between an angel—a being connected to the very creation of the universe—appearing at random and extremely advanced tech being hidden underground, I think we're in over our heads. Here's what's going to happen. We didn't find anything on this expedition. After we leave, we just bury the entrance to these ruins."

"What are you talking about, Lady Lilith? I mean, I'm an idiot, so I don't know the specifics, but even I can tell this is one hell of a find. I'm all for heading back to the hideout, but if we bury this, Lady Astaroth's gonna tear us a new one for sure."

I figured Lilith would be thrilled finding new technology, but something's wrong with her today.

"I would be fine if the worst thing that happened was us getting chewed out by Astaroth. Let me explain this in a way even a meathead like you can understand. The folks who built these ruins decided to make floating light sources for the ridiculous reason that 'it'd be inconvenient to lose light during an earthquake.' There's tech on Earth that lets you power appliances with electromagnetic fields in lieu of power cords, but that's still years away from practical use. We've also got nothing that can make this sort of thing float for decades, maybe even centuries. Do you get it now? Whatever lived here had technology more advanced than anything humanity has ever developed."

Lilith explains her concerns with a deathly serious expression.

"And? That really doesn't make this any easier for me to get a handle on. I mean, Lady Lilith, you've got lots of advanced tech, but without your tentacles, a random stray cat can make you cry."

"Sh-shut up. We're not talking about me right now! The gap in technology is the gap in power between species. We're going to run into trouble if the country we invade ends up being stronger than us."

Lilith is clearly not having my attitude, going as far as to deploy a single tentacle to slap me on the cheek.

Sure, the whole reason I was sent to this planet as a spy was to determine the locals' level of advancement.

So to some extent, I can understand what Lilith's saying, but...

Right at that moment—

"Huh? What's that? Something weird just grew out of Lady Lilith!"

Seeing the tentacle emerge from Lilith's lab coat, Rose lets out a yelp of surprise.

"...Oh, um, sorry about that, Patrasche, but I'm busy trying to explain something important to Six..."

As Lilith says this, looking like she's at a loss on how to respond...

"I remember seeing those wiggly silver things back when I was a kid!"

......

"You know, I've wanted to ask this for a while, but I've been restraining myself. Patrasche, just who the hell are you?"

Lilith's tone is as quiet as her expression is serious.

"I'm Patrasche, the Mounting Gorilla."

"Okay, I got that. Can we put that weird role-play aside for a minute? Tell me who you really are!"

Having had her introduction interrupted, Patrasche just removes the fursuit head with a soft *plomp*.

"Okay then, to properly reintroduce myself... I'm the boss's subordinate and Chimera, Rose. It's a pleasure to meet you, Lady Lilith!"

Seeing Rose emerge from the fursuit, Lilith stares with her mouth agape.

"...Wait, hold on. Just wait. Six, isn't Rose the...?"

"I *did* include her in my report, you know. She's the one who can get stronger by taking on the properties of whatever she eats—a future mutant candidate and current Combat Agent Recruit, Rose."

Our explanation has Lilith cradling her head and squatting on the floor.

"Wait, what the hell is going on?! I really don't understand this at all! None of it! If this Rose is the Chimera, then who was the one who showed me his junk?"

Oh, that's what she doesn't get.

Lilith thought Russell was the Chimera I mentioned in my reports.

"Are you serious, Lady Lilith? My reports were pretty clear that Rose is a girl."

"Well, sure, that's what they said! But still!"

Rose looks puzzled as the conversation leaves her far behind.

"Just to verify. Miss Chimera, do you have a penis?"

"Uh, I'm sorry, Lady Lilith. Until a few seconds ago, you reminded me a lot of my grandpa, but can I please take that back?"

Lilith hurriedly shakes her head in response to Rose's complete rejection of her.

"Wait, hang on. Listen, will you, Miss Chimera? I have a good reason for asking..."

"Russell showed off his junk to Lady Lilith while he was dressed in women's clothing, so she thought sex and gender were trivial matters for Chimeras."

"I have a hard time thinking of Russell as a fellow Chimera..."

"So Patrasche is Rose, as well as the Chimera from the reports. And you were raised in a facility like this one when you were a kid... and you've seen super-mechanical things that look like my tentacles."

"Yes, that about sums it up."

Lilith finally understands after Rose and I explain.

"I wish you would've just introduced yourself as Rose to begin with. That way, I wouldn't have gotten all confused... I mean, what sort of weird name is Patrasche...?"

Seemingly exhausted from the recent exchange, Lilith slumps her shoulders with a sigh.

"It's not exactly persuasive when we try telling people not to use false names. After all, Lady Lilith, your real surname is Yasuda."

"D-don't mention 'Yasuda'! You know you're forbidden from calling people by their real names once you join Kisaragi! But either way, we're getting out of here! Now! Whatever made that groaning noise might be headed our way!"

I don't know when that rule was implemented, but Yasuda barks out orders, her face turning a bright shade of red.

As Lilith blushes at being addressed by her actual name, someone tugs at her lab coat.

Rose, looking really odd without her fursuit head, stares straight at the little scientist.

"Lady Lilith, I think I might know this place. The voice we're hearing doesn't actually belong to anything scary."

She can't tell how she could know such a thing.

At least, that's what her expression suggests.

"Lady Lilith and Boss, you can return and wait at the hideout. I'll go check deeper in," offers Rose, smiling shyly to reassure us.

7

Thanks to a certain someone's depth charge, many of the mysterious floating lamps have been shattered, leaving the halls in these ruins dimly lit.

The wreckage of something is lying on its side at my feet...

"Hey, Rose, this might be the place you grew up in, right? The person who wrecked it is standing right there. You're welcome to hit her if you want."

"W-wait a second, Six! It's not like you thought we'd find a ruin like this inside that giant lizard's lair!"

The fact that Lilith and I are more talkative than usual is just part of the fun.

There's no way that a Supreme Leader and a Combat Agent from an evil organization can run on home, leaving a girl to fend for herself in here.

We managed to convince Rose not to go alone and have resumed our survey of the ruins.

"Um, Boss, Lady Lilith, you don't need to keep going if this is too much. You two get twitchy every time we find something odd, but for some reason, I'm not afraid of any of it. I should be fine on my own."

Rose continues leading us along the sparsely lit hallway.

Using Rose's tiny back as a marker, we continue deeper into these ruins, which reverberate with the creepy groaning.

"...You know, looking at the wreckage strewn everywhere, it doesn't seem like this stuff fell apart naturally. Just so we're clear, my depth charge wasn't the cause, either. This junk has been this way since way before that. These are the remains from some sort of battle."

"Hey, Rose, don't believe a word of what she's saying. She's always making baseless statements of one kind or another."

As I ignore Lilith's murderous gaze, Rose lets out a soft chuckle.

Despite her claims to the contrary, no doubt Lilith feels a bit guilty, which explains why she's still tagging along, complaining under her breath, even though she was petrified earlier.

"Lady Lilith, honestly, you do remind me of my grandpa," says Rose affectionately.

Unused to the syrupy sensation this elicits, Lilith turns away to avoid Rose's eyes.

We eventually arrive at a giant door deep inside the ruins.

Still wary of the groaning and rumbling from within, we open it and find a glass case that I swear I've seen somewhere before.

Yeah, I'm pretty sure that's the one we found in the neighboring kingdom of Toris.

The same one Russell had been sealed in...

"Look at this, Six! This device is used to gestate dangerous organics inside this glass tube! Specifically, stuff like pretty-boy homunculi or maybe someone's clone! Let's have Alice analyze it and make a second and third Astaroth and Belial! We can have a bunch of sweet, freshly born Astaroths pamper and take care of us."

Lilith responds much like I did when I first saw one of these.

"Um, I don't mean to interrupt, Lady Lilith, but...this is probably where I slept..."

Rose apologizes while Lilith continues gushing over the device. "Of course, I knew that. This is what you'd call a 'scientist joke'... Six, what are you looking at, exactly? If you have something you want to say, I'll listen to it later. Just...leave me alone for now."

As I watch her with a smirk, Lilith blushes and begins her survey.

The two of us walk in silence for a bit.

"Lady Lilith, do you have something to say?"

"Six, look at him. No doubt he's spent ages guarding this place. To stand here, obeying his creator's orders even as his body falls apart... A certain rebellious android could stand to learn a thing or two from him."

Sprawled out in front of us is a human-shaped robot, the source of that eerie rumbling, though its arms and legs have been destroyed.

I'd peg it at about three meters tall.

I don't know what it's made of, but even I can tell lead bullets wouldn't do much.

"Is this the thing you were afraid of, Lady Lilith?"

"Sh-shut up! You refused to explore deeper, too."

Rose returns to us after wandering around the room.

"This is Mr. Tomekichi, the gardener robot."

""Mr. Tomekichi.""

As her words completely wreck the dystopian mood in the room, Lilith and I can't help but repeat them.

"I don't know what a gardener robot is, but this golem is Mr. Tomekichi. His name popped into my head for some reason."

"*...Lady Lilith, what should we do with Mr. Tomekichi? Should we take him back to the hideout and repair him?*"

"*No, no. Even I can't repair a Mr. Tomekichi I've just seen for the first time. I may be a scientific genius, but I don't know how an alien robot is constructed.*"

As though hearing our whispered conversation, Rose shakes her head gently.

"Actually, since there's no more garden to tend, Mr. Tomekichi would like to retire. He isn't able to reach the switch on his back without his arms, so he'd appreciate it if you could do it for him."

"Huh...you can understand him...?"

Rose and Lilith circle around to Mr. Tomekichi's giant back to press the deactivation button.

While they do the honors, I decide to take a look around the ruins to see if there isn't something of value left lying around...

A map on the wall catches my eye.

Approaching and touching it, I notice it's not made of paper but some sort of petrochemical plastic.

"Six, what are you looking at? We've finished granting Mr. Tomekichi's retirement request."

Turning toward Lilith, I see Rose with her hands together, offering a little prayer for the now-immobile Mr. Tomekichi.

She's a good kid, but I wish she'd taken off the entire fursuit and not just the head.

...Anyway, the gardener robot (Mr. Tomekichi), these mysterious ruins, and an ancient super-culture...

"Lady Lilith, can I just quit thinking?"

"It's not like I ever had any expectations for you in that area anyway. Leave this sort of thing to Alice and me...but never mind that. This map..."

Looking refreshed, Rose joins us in studying the map.

"Boss, let's head back to the hideout. It's just a hunch, but I feel like there's nothing left here. I have no idea why I know this, but..."

It seems like Rose is remembering bits and pieces, but I guess she still can't sort out the important details.

"Oh, this map..."

Rose suddenly points at the item that's captured our attention.

"This! This seems to be the place where they found me. I'm not sure how I know this, but these are the ruins I was found in, and this is one of our summer homes."

These ruins appear to be stirring up all sorts of memories.

What do you mean, "summer home"? Aren't you a Chimera?

Or maybe she was a pretty well-off noble in the Chimera Kingdom?

"...Lady Lilith, you're smart, right? You get along with her pretty well. Can I leave figuring out her identity to you? There's just way too much Rose backstory, and I can feel my mind slipping away."

"You lost your mind a long time ago. And you're really going to push another thing on me, even though I don't know her nearly as well...?"

Rose begins tagging the map with the marker we'd been using for tic-tac-toe.

"So to recap: She was born here, and she was asleep in the summer home. When she woke up, someone had reduced this place—her home—to ruins. Meanwhile, Rose herself is suffering from amnesia..."

"...Aren't you the one who wrecked this place, Lady Lilith?"

"My depth charge wouldn't do this much damage! I-it's true! Besides, there wasn't much left of it anyway! I swear! Quit looking at me like that!"

I suppose it's enough of a discovery to learn that this wreckage-strewn ruin is where Rose was born and raised.

Just then, Rose interrupts our conversation.

"I remember there being a lot more machines in here... There should have been a Mr. Kikuzo, the giant-lizard gate guard... How did anyone get in before Lady Lilith stopped Mr. Kikuzo? And who were they?"

This new detail is another blow to Lilith's heart.

"Well, what are you planning to do, Lady Lilith? Not only did you wreck this amnesiac little Chimera's home, but that lizard you killed? That was Mr. Kikuzo."

"Wh-why don't we try phrasing it this way? Mr. Kikuzo's mission was to guard this place until Rose returned. He was defeated in the line of duty...... Once we get back to the hideout, I'll treat you to a ton of Japanese junk food! Can you find it in your heart to forgive me, Rose?"

"I don't know what Japanese junk food is, but that sounds good to me!"

Although she doesn't know what it is, Rose pieces together that Lilith is talking about food, so she eagerly agrees.

I feel a bit bad for Mr. Kikuzo being worth less than junk food, but from Rose's perspective, Lilith's right in that he actually did complete his mission. She thanks Lilith for retiring him like she did with Mr. Tomekichi.

Subjected to her thanks, my loner, shut-in boss, who's only accustomed to being reviled, shuffles her feet in discomfort…

8

The next morning.

Alice greets us as we return to the hideout after spending the previous evening in the ruins.

"You delinquents are finally home, huh? The ruins were only a short trip away. Why the hell did the survey take so long that you're *just* getting home?"

Alice lets loose with the venom as soon as she opens her mouth, but after a closer look at us, she tilts her head quizzically.

The focus of her gaze is an oddly satisfied-looking Rose as well as Lilith, who's sporting the opposite expression.

"Yo, Six, Rose looks like the few brain cells she had left trickled out of her head overnight, while Lady Lilith looks even gloomier than usual. What exactly happened out there?"

I recount the whole story from the beginning…

"Well, that sure sounds like a pain in the ass. So Rose got some of her memories back, and she marked five spots on the map. One of them is the ruin where they found her. Another is the one you explored yesterday, and yet another is the one we recently dealt with in Toris. As for the rest…this one's where the Demon Lord's got his headquarters, right smack where his castle is."

Alice pores over the map we brought back.

"…Huh, seriously? So the Demon Lord took over one of her summer homes or bases? Considering her daily pronouncements that humanity is the enemy, could she be…?"

"Ohhh! Wait, Boss, you've got the wrong idea there! I'm not a demon! I mean, yes, Mr. Russell, who's also a Chimera, decided to side with the Demon Lord, but for us, there actually isn't a fine distinction between demons and humans…"

As Rose anxiously provides an explanation, Alice gives her a look of pity.

"Don't worry about it. No one's going to suspect someone as simple as you of being a spy. If anything, the fact that your summer home was ransacked means it's probably more accurate to say that our competitor, the Demon Lord, is occupying one of your properties."

Rose lets out a sigh of relief at Alice's calm summary of the situation.

"Putting that aside for a moment, are you done being Patrasche?"

Hearing Alice's question, a smile lights Rose's satisfied expression.

"Well, it's like, now that I know so much about myself, the whole life of gluttony and sloth under a new grandpa feels wrong to me… Also, I want to pay back Boss and the others for helping me find out about my past… I figured I could do that by working for Kisaragi…"

Rose chuckles shyly, scratching at the back of her head, but I'm pretty sure the whole "gluttony and sloth" part was wrong even before the remembering-the-past bit.

…As Rose laughs uncomfortably, Alice approaches her.

"Looks like you've gotten over a lot that was troubling you. Welcome to the Kisaragi Corporation. We're an evil organization, so we don't think twice about ruthless acts of villainy, nor do we forgive betrayal. We crush our enemies and don't give a damn about justice. However..."

Lately, this android, who's supposed to be the product of cold pragmatism, is starting to show a lot more emotion.

"...at Kisaragi, we value our comrades. If the Demon Lord has taken up residence in your home, we'll get it back for you, no matter how long it takes."

She's made a flat-out declaration, even as our available forces are about to dwindle, what with Lilith and myself eventually returning to Earth.

"...Whoa, whoa, Miss Alice. You need to remember I'm heading back to Earth. The forces at your disposal are gonna take a serious hit. C'mon, say it. Go ahead and say it. It'll be so much easier if you have Mr. Six at your side."

"That's true. If we had Six, we could take over the Demon Lord's Castle in three years. Without you, it'll take us three years."

Huh, she's being awfully honest...

"...Hold on, you just gave the same amount of time. If you have me, you could probably do it in about a year, don't you think?"

"Eh, your presence only moves up the timeline by about three days. So you can relax, leave Rose to me, and head home. Earth is where you're needed right now."

Rose smiles in amusement at the exchange between Alice and me.

Lilith, who's been sitting quietly, finally speaks up.

"...I must admire your tenacity, Miss Chimera. In comparison, I don't have a single positive to speak of."

Lilith looks as though she's put her past failures behind her.

"I've read all about you in the reports. You've been waiting this whole time, patiently helping out the kingdom with information about your past as a lure, right? And now that you've finally got a hint, are you planning to wait another three years?"

Lilith's words seem to have caught Rose off guard.

"As of today, you're officially a member of our family. As Alice noted earlier, the Kisaragi Corporation is an outstanding company that cares for its employees."

The bit about being a company that cares for its employees is news to me, but it seems our ordinarily useless boss has evolved (for the moment) into one of Kisaragi's rightful Supreme Leaders.

"Very well, Combat Agent Recruit Rose. Welcome to the Kisaragi Corporation! Allow me to welcome you on behalf of the Supreme Leaders. And…"

Like Alice, Lilith appears to be in a better mood than usual, smiling happily at Rose.

"You've got somewhere you want to go, right? You have something you want to learn, right? No need to be modest. Nothing is impossible for the Kisaragi Corporation!"

Having seemingly put the past in the past, after peppering Rose with a series of questions, Lilith approaches her with arms outstretched.

Having spent a long time being treated like an unwanted outsider in this kingdom, Rose probably isn't used to this sort of treatment.

With no family other than her grandpa, she probably didn't have anyone she could turn to.

She's likely never had anyone celebrate her birthday before.

If that weren't the case, she wouldn't so overwhelmed.

Tearing up, Rose comes to a decision, her cheeks faintly flushed.

"L-Lady Lilith… U-um, that is, my wish is to go visit the Demon Lord. I want to ask him why he's living in one of the ruins. And I want to ask what he knows about me!"

Hearing that, Lilith's face lights up in a wide grin.

"Very well. A talk with the Demon Lord, mm? Talking is one of my specialties!"

My socially awkward boss, who usually spends her days as a shut-in, makes a bold claim.

"What are you talking about, Lady Lilith? You get so flustered when a convenience store clerk asks if you want your bento box heated up that you reheat it at home instead."

"Sh-shut up, Six! What I'm going to do is conduct a Kisaragi Corporation–style discussion!"

Dismissing my observation, Lilith pushes back.

Seeing her behavior, Alice smiles teasingly.

"You sure about that, Lady Lilith? Even though you were so scared until now? The Demon Lord's Army is the real deal."

But not to be deterred...

"Quiet, Alice. Who do you think I am? I'm your creator and a Supreme Leader of the Kisaragi Corporation, Lilith the Black! What's one backwater Demon Lord compared to taking on the entire world?"

Despite being a chicken at heart, my boss fires back indignantly.

"...Um, Lady Lilith, we're just going there to talk, right?"

"That's right, Combat Agent Recruit Rose. We'll have a nice chat."

Contrary to Rose's concerned expression, Lilith is sporting a cocky grin.

"Come with me. We'll show this planet's natives and our competitors the true power of the Kisaragi Corporation!"

Even though she's ordinarily a coward, Lilith will do whatever it takes to help those she considers her friends when they're in trouble.

She's rude, conniving, and has few redeeming features as a boss, but everyone knows they can count on her for help.

"You sure about this, Lady Lilith? We're talking about a Demon Lord here. He's probably way tougher than an angel. This is one of those enemies you just can't beat if you're not the legendary Chosen One."

"And based on yesterday's survey, this planet's technology might actually be superior to ours. Are you prepared to move ahead with this anyway, Creator? I'm in if you are."

"…Why are you two so eager to undermine me when I've finally worked up some nerve? You know I'm shy. You realize that's why I always ended up losing steam during our stranger encounters, right, Six?"

"Of course, I'm aware of that. I've known you long enough. I also know the reason no one respects you is because, while you've got all the ability in the world when you're motivated, you give up so easily. That's why no one ever votes for you, Lady Lilith."

Despite her hostility toward the locals and her intention to drag me away from here, at heart, my boss is like me: someone who can't quite commit to being a true villain and, in her own twisted way, has a soft spot for people.

My boss, who falls silent at my remarks, is someone I can't quite hate because she's often so openly vulnerable.

"Yeah, you're right. I'm the most cowardly of the three Supreme Leaders. I'll even admit I make a lot of mistakes! …But you know what? I may make the most mistakes, but I've also got the most successes!"

That day, the boss I admire—one of the Supreme Leaders, Lilith the Black—commits to showing what she's really capable of.

1

The day after Lilith resolves to get things done.

All the Combat Agents have assembled in front of our newly constructed hideout.

Few gathered here have any idea why they've been summoned.

"Very well, all of you, allow me to explain why I've ordered you to abandon the front lines and gather here today. So long as you follow my directions, I'll forgive that none of you came to greet me, a Supreme Leader of the Kisaragi Corporation. I am, after all, a generous and gracious boss. I'm not remotely hurt that you've excluded me from your activities, nor do I hold that against you."

Standing atop a hastily erected dais, Lilith raises her voice to address the troops.

It's pretty obvious from the barbs scattered throughout her remarks that she is, in fact, nursing a grudge, but no one points this out.

Why? Because Lilith has her game face on today.

The more senior the agent, the more they put their trust in Lilith when she's serious.

"No doubt there are some of you who have seen her around. And no doubt some of you have spoken to her before. But today, I'll introduce you all to a new Combat Agent Recruit... She's none other than the Chimera girl standing next to me, Rose!"

"To everyone I've never met, nice to meet you! I'm Rose, a Chimera and Combat Agent Recruit. I'm looking forward to working with all of you!"

Rose, forced to stand beside Lilith, blushes nervously as she calls out to the gathering.

As a pattering of applause echoes from the agents, Lilith holds her hand up for silence.

"Now, obviously, I have not assembled you all merely to introduce you to a new recruit. The Kisaragi Corporation's leadership is diverse. There is a ruthless ice queen who considers agents expendable. We also have a meathead flame warrior who insists that Combat Agents exist to die in battle and that those who aren't weak will end up surviving. As for me..."

Lilith takes a meaningful pause after insulting her colleagues.

"I, as the Supreme Leader most concerned with the welfare of our Combat Agents, will never abandon or betray you, our precious agents. No doubt you are all aware of this already!"

Whispers ripple across the gathered agents.

"When I went to Lady Lilith after spilling ketchup on Lady Astaroth's uniform, she shooed me away and told me it wasn't her problem."

"One time, she goaded me into playing a practical joke on Lady Belial, telling me it'd be fun to tease a beautiful boss. She sold me out the moment we got caught."

Lilith's brow twitches, as though she's heard the subdued griping.

"It seems some of you have something to say. Speak up, then! I'll make note of your faces and names. You know my intelligence! I never forget a face. I'll be sure to remember them until the next round of HR evaluations!" says the shitty boss, not even batting an eye at her abuse of authority.

That's the sort of thing that guarantees no one votes for her in the various surveys.

"I will ignore our differing perspectives for now. What I wanted to point out...was the fact that when any of you Combat Agents are harmed by an outside enemy, I will always and immediately strike out to avenge you."

This time, no one breathes so much as a word of disagreement.

As the name *Lilith the Black* indicates, the reason she maintains something of a following despite her completely rotten personality is the fact that the moment a subordinate is victimized by the enemy, Lilith always pays them back in kind.

She's a petty, petulant, and often useless antisocial character with flaws aplenty, but no one here denies her vindictive loyalty to her subordinates.

"...Now, that should be enough to clue you in to why you've been assembled here today, yes?"

....

"Hey, did you follow that?"

"Yeah... So we're here to have a welcoming party. We're gonna have a party with that Chimera girl, I guess."

"Oh, gotcha. Guess I'll head off to the woods and grab us a mokemoke."

"A welcoming party? Pretty thoughtful for an antisocial boss. Still not planning on voting for her, though."

Lilith's face flushes, as it appears the point has sailed right over the heads of the assembled agents.

"Why are you Combat Agents all so uniformly stupid?! Hey, Six! Tell them what we're about to do!"

This is why dealing with the lowest level of lackeys is such a headache…

"Let me make it clear for the dimmest of you lot. Rose is a Chimera who can acquire the abilities of whatever she eats. That means you all need to use your Evil Points to gather rare ingredients…"

"No! Wrong! Forget it! Why am I surrounded by idiots?! Listen up, all of you: The Demon Lord's Army has taken over and occupied a place near and dear to Rose's heart!"

"Huh?! Um, no, that's not it, Lady Lilith. We don't even know if they've taken it over. I was just thinking I'd remember more about my past if we visited the spots I marked on the map…"

Lilith pretends not to hear Rose as she clarifies in a soft voice.

"Listen up, Combat Agents! She's the kind of pretty girl you all love! Our new pretty-girl Chimera recruit has had a place dear to her heart taken from her, and now she's suffering for it! Even you morons know what comes next, right?!"

"""Yeaaaaaaaaaaaaaaaaaaaaaaaaaaaaaaaaaaaaah!"""

Seems it was clear enough for them this time.

"We're heading to the Demon Lord's Castle! Combat Agents, gather your weapons! Tiger Man, organize the rabble!"

Lilith boldly issues her orders before the excited throng of Combat Agents.

"To the Demon Lord's Castle! They won't know what hit 'em!"

"Lady Lilith! What happened to talking it out?!"

Rose's objection is swallowed by the surge of cheers erupting from the Combat Agents—

"I will now hand out your assignments for this mission. First, Tiger Man! Lead the Combat Agents and raid the Demon Lord's Kingdom! During this operation, you are to ignore any movements from the enemy nation of Toris! Even if they take possession of some territory, we can reclaim it later. If we end this war in a single day, they won't even have time to invade."

"So...we're doing decoy work as usual nyeow?"

I wish he wouldn't do that whole meowing thing while saluting with a straight face.

"Exactly. Your role is to draw the enemy to you. But instead of the usual border skirmish, this time, you're going to attack the Demon Lord's Kingdom directly. You'll need to cause a huge commotion. Can I count on you?"

"Leave it to me, Meows Lilith! It's been a while since I've led an all-out assault! I can't wait!"

Tiger Man wears a cocky smile and cracks his knuckles.

"We're counting on you, Tiger Man! And if you call me 'Meows Lilith' again, you're getting tentacled!"

"Won't happen again, Meows Lilith!"

The tentacles immediately grab Tiger Man, hauling him into the air, and he begins meowing out his apologies.

"Next, Combat Agent Six! You and Rose will come with me."

"Roger, Lady Lilith! So we're your escort, huh?"

"I'll do my best to protect you, Lady Lilith!"

Rose balls up a fist, prompting a faint smile from Lilith.

Alice rests her shotgun against her shoulder, looking rather pleased as she watches Lilith.

"And as for you, Alice..."

"I'm coming with you, of course. It's too dangerous to leave my useless creator without supervision."

Alice interjects before Lilith can give her orders.

Lilith doesn't bother responding. She just wears a happy smile.

...And at that moment.

"Wait a second, Lady Lilith. We're attacking the Demon Lord's

Castle this time, right? Then we'd like to participate in the assault instead of just the diversion!"

"In that case, I wanna go, too."

"Yeah. Why does Six always get special treatment anyway?!"

"Damn thug, it's unfair he gets the nice gigs because he's been around longer! Switch places with me, dammit!"

The dime-a-dozen Combat Agents assigned to be a diversion begin whining.

Lilith tilts her head a moment, a troubled expression crossing her features...

"W-well, if that's what you all want, I suppose you can take over for Six..."

"Wait, what are you saying, Lady Lilith? There's no way these weaklings can take over for me, someone who's served you for so many years. It's not like these obnoxious lackeys are useful for anything but a diversion anyway. It's not good leadership to flip-flop on a decision you just made."

I quickly interject before Lilith can finish speaking.

Hearing my tirade, the weakling agents start jeering at me.

"Ahhh, all right, all right. Six, the rest of you, calm down! I understand your feelings. If all of you are so eager to come with me, you're all welcome to join! Oh, but Agent Ten, not you. Since you can fly an airplane, you're responsible for carrying me to the destination."

Lilith is unable to suppress a smirk at having her subordinates fawn over her.

"...Wait, a plane? What sort of mission are you planning if you need Agent Ten to pilot a plane?"

I can't help but feel a tinge of anxiety.

Seems like the other agents feel the same way, with them all going quiet to hear Lilith's response.

"Ah, right... Let me give you the key details of the plan. The Combat Agents led by Tiger Man will pick a big fight with the Demon

Lord's Army. They'll make it as messy and elaborate as possible. Don't worry about the points needed to request weapons. Go crazy. I'll cover the point cost. The weapons and ammo are on me today, so don't hold back!"

Everyone lets out a cheer at Lilith's show of confidence.

Hold on, they get to use as many weapons as they want, and Lilith's gonna pay for it? I'm starting to want to go with them...

"As you draw the attention of the Demon Lord's Army, Agent Ten will pilot a plane to drop the four of us off in the middle of enemy territory. While the enemy lacks modern weaponry, they do have this so-called magic technology, which means they'll likely have antiair weaponry. Agent Ten will retreat as soon as we drop. He'll then return to the Grace-Demon Lord's Army border and provide air support for Tiger Man's forces."

...Upon hearing this, everyone falls into stunned silence while Agent Ten nods in acknowledgment.

Diving into the middle of the enemy headquarters from the sky.

Having heard this idiotic plan proposed by the supposed genius Lilith, the Combat Agents, who had been yelling at me a moment earlier, turn away.

"...Well, then. We're counting on you, Lady Lilith. I'll go on the decoy mission, so please come back safely."

"Hold it, Six, this is a mission tailor-made for you. You're the agent with the best survival skills, after all."

"Yes. Six has known Lady Lilith the longest. For something big like taking out the Demon Lord, I think you, who came to this planet first, should do the honors."

"Heh, you know we were just kidding. There's no way we'd try to grab the spoils out from under you after all the work you've put in."

The Combat Agents change their tune at the drop of a hat.

"What the hell, you bastards?! One of you, trade places with me! I mean, why the hell do I always get the dangerous stuff? Screw that! You know I was sent here when teleporting was most unstable, right?!"

My desperate attempts at negotiation all fall on deaf ears.

"Wh-what's wrong, everyone? You can volunteer to come with me if you want!"

2

"Well nyeow, Lady Lilith, we wish you success!"

We watch the ground forces led by Tiger Man snap off salutes to Lilith before heading out.

It will take a while until Tiger Man and the Combat Agents engage the Demon Lord's Army.

Since we'd easily overtake them in our plane regardless of how fast they push their land vehicles, we have nothing to do but hurry up and wait until the decoys engage the enemy's main force.

In the end, the ones left are Lilith, Alice, Rose, me, and the pilot, Combat Agent Ten.

Though we have plenty of time, this is a sortie Lilith threw together in a hurry, so there's no harm in taking a moment to sort out the specifics.

"…The plan is as I explained earlier. We will be offering Tiger Man as a precious sacrifice. He will catch the Demon Lord—probably while he's gazing up at the sky and cackling, or something—and then, he'll rip out his jugular. I understand the description makes this sound rather risky, but my presence will make up for that."

The risk is that you *came up with it.* I barely manage to swallow the words before they come out of my mouth.

"The ideal situation would be a precise drop by Combat Agent Ten. Demon Lords tend to live at the tops of their castles anyway. If there's no antiaircraft fire, we'll have Ten bring us in as close as possible and drop us at the top floor. Then, we crash through the windows and kill the Demon Lord. Problem solved!"

"No, don't solve the problem, Lady Lilith! I want to talk to the Demon Lord!"

Rose's objection reminds Lilith of the original objective.

"N-now, on the other hand!"

She wants to pretend the last line didn't happen.

"If the antiair fire is too thick and we can't get to the castle, then we'll release multiple parachutes as dummies. We'll then drop last toward the rear of the castle. There'll be a rain of parachutes falling into the enemy capital, where the Demon Lord's Castle is. Obviously, the enemy combatants in the city will scatter to respond to the various drop points. Once we spread out the enemy forces in this way...we'll strong-arm our way into the Demon Lord's Castle from the rear, heading to the top floor! Then, all we have to do is rid ourselves of the Demon Lord as soon as we find him. Problem solved!"

"Again, please don't solve the problem, Lady Lilith! I keep telling you we're going to talk to him. I mean..."

Rose cocks her head slightly.

"I mean, we may have found the Demon Lord's Castle, but how are we going to get inside? We need to clear the fog surrounding it using the treasure from the Tower of Duster..."

...What's she talking about all of a sudden?

Why are we discussing an RPG?

Lilith seems to be thinking the same thing, looking at Rose quizzically.

"Once the fog clears, we have to place the sorcerer stones from each of the Elite Four into the towers arrayed north, south, east, and west of the Demon Lord's Castle. Once we do that..."

"The barrier around the castle disappears, and the path to the Demon Lord opens up, right? Yeah, we know."

Rose's eyes go wide in surprise.

"Wait, you knew all this, Boss? I heard this was pretty much top secret…"

Clearing the fog with a treasure, removing the barrier with items taken from beating the Elite Four—these are all RPG clichés.

Alice then opens her mouth.

"Yo, Six. Remember this kingdom's prophecy had a divinely guided Chosen One eventually taking out the Demon Lord. I'm sure you've forgotten because you're all brawn and no brain, but we conquered that Tower of Duster for the Chosen One."

…Did we really?

"But while we were taking that tower's treasure, Whatever of the Wind caught the Chosen One in a Random Teleport spell, and the two vanished without a trace…"

Oh, now that she mentions it, I do kinda remember something like that…

"…Uh, so what are we going to do? Can't we have an outcome where I awaken to some mysterious power and become the new Chosen One?"

Lilith rushes through her question, reacting like I did the first time I heard about the prophecy of the Chosen One.

"Well, just forget about the prophecy. The Chosen One's gone, and Whatever of the Wind has vanished, too. Which means we can't use the clichéd solution in either case… I mean, Six, you've beaten three of their Elite Four to date, but did you recover their sorcerer stones or whatever?"

Now that Alice mentions it, I don't remember collecting those drops.

…No, wait a minute.

"When I first beat Heine of the Flames, I got a rock like that, remember? The one Heine got all teary-eyed about and said she'd do anything to get back. The one I told her I'd consider handing over if she posed for those pervy pictures."

"You did what? That's going a bit too far, don't you think?"

Yeah, I did grab that sorcerer stone.

"Good job. You remembered something for once. Just to jog your memory about what happened after, you ended up not giving it back to her and blew it up using a land mine. Right in front of Heine's eyes, at that."

...I don't remember that one, actually.

Lilith and Rose shoot me disgusted looks.

"Besides, Gadalkand of the Earth didn't have a sorcerer stone, and Russell of the Water is using his as we speak to deal with the kingdom's water shortage. Even if we could get three out of four, Whatever of the Wind being missing means we're out of options. We don't have a way to go the clichéd route."

According to Alice's assessment, we've only got one alternative.

Just then, Lilith, who has been listening till now, grins.

"...See? Since we're an evil organization, we can't take the easy path. Besides, we don't need to do things the 'right' way."

Lilith brushes aside the very idea.

"Yes, the Kisaragi way is to go against the norm. We'll also resort to our twisted methods to take out the Demon Lord!"

"Like I keep saying, Lady Lilith, we can't take him out—!"

"—It's about time. Are you all ready to go?"

It's been about half a day since Tiger Man and company set off.

Combat Agent Ten, who has been quietly tuning into the conversation with his eyes closed and his arms across his chest, suddenly speaks up, gesturing at the plane with his thumb as if to tell us to hop aboard.

"...S-sure, we're ready, but... Say, Combat Agent Ten, despite the fact that you're a rank-and-file agent like Six, you've got...a really unique personality."

"Not at all. I'm just one of your average, everyday Combat Agents."

Without much daily contact with Combat Agents other than me, Lilith appears to have taken an interest in Ten.

She seems to suddenly remember something and lets out a soft "Ah!"

"Oh yeah, Combat Agent Ten! The kingdom's princess really chewed me out because of your bullshit!"

As Lilith yells at him, Ten breaks out in a roguish grin.

"Well now, there's too many things I could think of to feel guilty about to recall any specific incident. I'm a Combat Agent for an evil organization. Evil antics are my daily bread…"

"That's not it at all! I'm a villain, too! If it was ordinary villainy, I'd be praising you. But your case is different! You tried to poop in the princess's room! Why did that even cross your mind?!"

…Huh, Rose is looking at Ten as though observing something beyond her comprehension.

"Oh, come on now, Lady Lilith. I may be the survivor of countless battlefields, and I may have done all sorts of reckless things in the past, but even I have to poop after eating. Or are you telling me not to defecate? If you asked me to kill a dragon or refrain from pooping… well, I'd go kill the dragon without a second thought. I'm sorry, but that's just who I am."

"I'm telling you to crap in the toilet!"

I wish I could listen to Lilith and Ten's idiotic conversation for a while longer, but it's getting to be that time.

Alice quickly hops into the aircraft—or more precisely, the giant transport plane—which was ordered using a boatload of Lilith's Evil Points.

"Just get going already. Ten's as dumb as usual, but why are you going on about poop, Lady Lilith? You showed a weird fixation with the Sky King's poop, too, but this is messed up even for me."

"Fine, I shouldn't have brought this up in the first place. This conversation's over. But I have one last thing to say to Combat Agent Ten—POOP IN THE TOILET!"

Lilith then climbs into the aircraft, but one look at her face tells me that she had a lot more she wanted to say. Once he confirms everyone's aboard, Ten starts up the plane and takes off.

3

"We're really flying, Boss! Look, look, there's a supopocchi fighting a mokemoke over there! Let's stop by on the way home, capture the one that loses, and boil it!"

Excited by her first flight, Rose looks down at the ground and kicks up a fuss.

"See, Six? This is how natives should react to superior technology. That's the reaction I was looking for."

Apparently, this is what Lilith had in mind with her Lilithification plans, and she smiles contentedly.

"...Hey, mind if I butt in? Isn't that the Sky King or whatever?"

Alice has been surveying our surroundings, and we look in the direction she's pointing.

"Yeah, that's the Sky King. You know, at that size, I bet we wouldn't go hungry for a long time..."

"It's supposed to be the Guardian Beast. Don't eat it."

I make sure to quip to Rose after her disturbing remark, but...

I can't really tell from this distance, but it looks like someone on the ground is getting chased by the Sky King.

Probably some idiot who raided the Sky King's lair.

We're too far away to get a clear look at the poor soul being pursued, but there's something familiar about that silhouette.

"Yo, what's going on, Six? You're staring so intently into the distance."

"Well, it looks like the Sky King's chasing someone or something... Should we go help?"

If we weren't in the middle of a mission, we could do a good deed in hopes of getting a reward.

"...Unless you've stolen something important or are carrying something shiny, the Sky King won't bother with you. And if you've stolen something, it'll forgive you if you give it back. For shiny stuff, if you hide it under your clothes and hold it like it's really important to you, it'll eventually give up. If the Sky King is after somebody, it's totally that person's fault."

Rose's unexpectedly harsh assessment convinces me to let the strangely familiar stranger go it alone.

...And more importantly.

"Hey, Ten. Um, I've been wondering since earlier, but are you using a controller from a game console to fly this plane?"

"Oh yeah. This is the sort of controller I'm most comfortable with. I used my own points to order it. So long as I have this in hand, I'm one of the best pilots in the world."

Wow, one of the best in the world. That's a lot of confidence.

"Glad to hear that. We're counting on you, Ten."

Alice approaches, her curiosity piqued by our exchange.

"If I didn't have to participate in the parachute drop, I'd do the piloting. Still, where'd you learn to fly like that? I know we're not supposed to dig into someone's past at Kisaragi, but I have to admit, I'm curious."

"Heh. It'd be better to talk about it after we're home safe... Well, the long and the short of it is that I grew up with a unique family and had to teach myself how to fly a plane."

......?

Wait, "a unique family"? What does that have to do with him teaching himself how to fly?

...Wait, he *taught himself*?

"We're approaching the drop zone. Looks like it's my time to shine. Heh, I love a good challenge!"

For some reason, rather than reassuring me, his confidence fills me with a sense of dread.

"All right, is everyone set? We're counting on you, Ten. Show us the skill that made you bravely volunteer when I took a shot in the dark and asked if anyone knew how to fly a plane... Everyone else, prepare for the drop!"

As a structure that appears to be the Demon Lord's Castle comes into view, tension begins building inside the plane.

...As the cabin grows quiet, I have a question I really need to ask.

"...Hey, Ten, I just can't get over the fact that you're using that game controller. You mentioned you taught yourself to fly... You don't mean that you taught yourself by playing *Lace Combat*, do you?"

I mean this as a joke, of course.

I asked because I wanted to use this as an opening for him to tell me where he learned to fly.

On average, most Combat Agents are dumb as dirt.

I can't shake the feeling there's something odd about one of them having a genuine pilot's license.

Ten laughs at my suggestion, though, as if I made a particularly funny joke.

Seeing his reaction, I relax a little.

"Okay, my bad. That was a stupid thing to ask."

My apology elicits a thin smile and a shrug from Ten.

"Yeah, no kidding. Who do you think I am? The first *Lace Combat*? Are you crazy? ...I learned from *Lace Combat Final*. That one had online matches and was really difficult. One time, I stole money from my sister's piggy bank, spent it on in-game items, and wound up as one of the top ten players in the world."

"Everyone, put on your parachutes, quick! Alice, do you think you can take the controls for a bit?"

"I can use my connector, but that'll cause problems with the parachute drop. It's safer to abandon this plane and get to the ground ASAP."

"Why's everyone suddenly so panicked? Did something happen?"

As the cabin becomes a beehive of activity, Rose alone remains calm.

"I told you! I TOLD YOU! Combat Agents are all morons! If he had an actual license, he wouldn't be a Combat Agent! That'd be obvious after thinking about it for a *second*! Dammit!"

"Calm down, Six. Leave this to me. With my trusty controller, I'm invincible. And I bought tons of prepaid cards to spend on in-game items, so there's no problem here."

As soon as I hear that, I kick open the plane door.

Lilith screams without a shred of hesitation:

"Deploy parachutes—!"

The Demon Lord's Kingdom is a vast wasteland dotted with a number of small deserts.

After landing in the middle of these vast wastelands...

"Th-thought we were gonna die...! If Ten makes it home, he's in for an earful!"

Actually, thinking about it, how the hell did he take off using a game controller?

"Is everyone safe? No one's hurt?"

"I'm okay! Actually, it was fun coming down from the sky!"

"Obviously, I'm fine. If there was a problem, this area would have been wiped out by my reactor."

Lilith checks on everyone present, and it seems there aren't any issues.

In fact, the problem is we still have a long way to go until we get to the Demon Lord's Castle.

I don't know where we landed exactly, but I do know we're deep in demon territory, which means our options are to either head toward the Demon Lord's Castle, vaguely visible in the distance, or decide the mission's a wash and beat a retreat...

Now on the ground, we can hear the distant sound of explosions in the background, probably from modern small-arms fire. Which must mean Tiger Man's started his attack.

"Alice, after confirming our current position, let's move to the closest hill."

Unfazed by this setback, Lilith quickly gives further orders.

"We're north-northwest of the Demon Lord's Castle. About fifteen klicks out. I've linked up with your satellite, Lady Lilith, but there aren't any hills nearby. I have found a group of hostiles heading this way, though."

"Oh, dang it! The enemy's already coming for us? Why did my perfect plan with layers and layers of schemes go wrong?"

"I think it's because you forgot to check Ten's qualifications."

A rock flies at me in response to my accurate feedback.

"Why does this always happen to me...? I mean, ordinarily, this is where my brilliant, brainy plan goes off without a hitch, allowing me to show off before canceling the widely hated order of dragging Six back to Earth, and then having everyone praise the wonders of Lilithification after I depart, isn't it?"

I'd like to think it's because she doesn't think things through enough on a day-to-day basis.

......Wait.

"Hey, Lady Lilith, what was that? Did you just say you're going to cancel Six's forced repatriation and leave him to continue serving as my partner?"

"Yeah, that's right! That's what I said! I mean, what choice do I have?! If it was just the greedy knight or that clingy woman, I'd take him back in a heartbeat. But rather than the cross-dressing Chimera, it was Patrasche who swayed me. And she happens to be attached to

Six and have a really heavy, tragic history. Of course I wouldn't hesitate to follow through!"

Hearing that, Alice stops moving.

"…You know, I think about this a lot, but the Kisaragi Supreme Leaders are all *tsundere*, aren't they?"

"Shut up, Six! At the very least, I am not a *tsundere*! I'm the honest and kind Lady Lilith!"

Rose fidgets a bit, happily listening to them bicker.

"I'm too dumb to get the full gist of what's going on, but does this mean the boss and Miss Alice can stay together because I like the boss?"

"Yes, that's right. But remember that's on my judgment alone! Hooray, Miss Chimera! When you get back to base, make sure you get Six and Alice to treat you to all sorts of goodies!"

Lilith's cheeks flush faintly.

…What should I do with this *tsundere* boss? I guess it wouldn't hurt for Alice and me to be a little nicer to her.

Just as I'm thinking up a scheme and Alice is staring blankly at the sky, evidently lost in thought…

"Mrrreow. Lady Lilith, do you copy? This is the Tigerrr Man Decoy Squad…over!"

Tiger Man's voice comes over Lilith's radio receiver.

"We've done a cerrrtain amount of damage to the Demon Lord's Arrrmeow, but the Sand King suddenly appurrred on the battlefield. Our currrent weaponry is insufficient, so I'm rrreturning to the hideout. Furrrthermore, the Demon Lord's Arrrmeow also retreated with the Sand King's appurrrance, so there's a high purrrobability you'll encounterrr the enemy if you're heading to the Demon Lord's Castle. This mission is a failurrrre. I suggest immeowdiate rrretreat…meow. Over."

……

The painful report completely spoils the mood.

Alice, who's been staring upward, shakes her head and shrugs her shoulders.

"...I guess I should've expected things to go south. Once Lady Lilith returns to Earth after having failed her mission, we'll get Lady Astaroth or Lady Belial over here... Well, I guess it's a win to have seen my creator be useful. The enemy units converging on this spot are probably the main forces of the Demon Lord's Army. Lady Lilith, have them send us another plane. This is the time to make a hasty retreat."

...As Alice says, I guess we can call it a win to have seen Lilith's soft side.

"Rose, you heard her. It might be a bit dangerous, but we're pulling back this time. Next time, we'll plan better and return after making the proper preparations. It might take a while, but we'll grant you your wish."

"A-all right! I mean, we tried to rush things too much this time, didn't we? Anyway, I got plenty of information from the survey of the ruins, so I'm plenty satisfied!"

As Rose smiles at my promise...

"This is Lilith. Negative on retreat. We will continue the mission. Tiger Man, your unit is cleared to retreat to the hideout. The Sand King's appearance was unexpected... No, actually, with the information at hand, I could've anticipated it. It's my fault. Sorry. Thanks for your efforts. Head on home. Over and out."

Lilith completely kills the mood over the radio.

4

"I know, I know. I'm well aware, given that I make plenty of mistakes. It's why everyone calls me the useless boss. And you, Combat Agent Six, are the one who's called me that most often."

We're in the middle of a wasteland without any cover in sight.

If we make our stand here, they'll undoubtedly spot us, even at a distance.

At the very least, our parachute drop must've been visible from the entire Demon Lord's Kingdom, and according to Alice, the Demon Lord's Army is converging on us.

Which means...

...not only are we going to face several thousand soldiers, but they'll be getting a steady stream of reinforcements.

"Are you serious, Lady Lilith? That's the core of the Demon Lord's Army! In effect, it's their entire military! See those dark-brown boobs up in front? That's one of the Demon Lord's Elite Four, Heine of the Flames."

Yes, at the head of the Demon Lord's Army, unmoving as though wary of us, stands Heine of the Flames, her arms crossed over her chest.

"Ah, one of the competition's leaders who you mentioned in your reports. I'm not afraid of a pair of tits. Size isn't everything. Mine are quite well shaped!"

My flat boss adds some irrelevant information as she and Alice ready themselves for combat without sparing another glance at the forces in front of us.

"...Um, Lady Lilith, what are you doing? Also, are you really planning to fight them?"

I can understand Rose's concerns.

"I'm just making preparations so that, in the worst case, I can go all out."

Their preparations aren't much.

They're just arranging the stockpile of heavy weapons sent over by the teleporter around Lilith.

"As for the second question on whether I actually mean to fight... Well, let my actions speak for themselves."

Surrounded by mortars on all sides, Lilith actually seems quite chipper.

What's going on? Is she just getting an adrenaline rush before battle?

This gloomy character isn't usually one to enjoy this sort of all-out brawl.

"Hey, Six, I'm starting to set up, so carry this next to Lady Lilith."

"...? Miss Alice, what's that?"

"This is a relay interface that lets people other than me create a satellite link. We'll take the cord from it and stick the end into one of Lady Lilith's holes."

"Phrasing! Alice, that phrasing is wrong on so many levels. Rose, don't take it in a weird way. My body has an interface device embedded in it through modification surgery so I can interact with machines like this. That's an important detail, so remember it. I have more openings on my body than most people. And I don't mean that in a sexual way."

While Lilith is busy digging her own grave, we continue readying ourselves for combat.

Lilith takes the countless cords stretching from the heavy weaponry, pulls them into her lab coat, and does *something* with them.

...What the heck is happening under her lab coat? I really want to know.

"Lady Lilith, should I help you with plugging in those cords?"

"No thanks. If I let you help, it's definitely going to end in tragedy. Specifically, a perverted tragedy."

Seeing countless unfamiliar heavy weapons, the Demon Lord's Army, with Heine at the helm, looks increasingly wary.

"Hey, Alice, shouldn't we stop this? I feel like it's going to end with a literal bang."

"I figure Lady Lilith's got a lot of pent-up frustration from having been away from you for so long. This spare-no-expense, overwhelming display of firepower doubles as stress relief. She's targeting the competition; let's just sit back and let her do her thing."

I suppose that sort of ruthless pragmatism is to be expected of an android with a heart of metal.

"...However, the points Lady Lilith had saved up were originally meant for the final battle on Earth. If she uses this much firepower on this planet, she's going to burn through her points and end up in the negatives after a volley or two."

As one of the Supreme Leaders of the Kisaragi Corporation, Lilith's got an insane number of Evil Points. She's probably earned enough just off the various terrible weapons she's invented over the years to rank first or second in Kisaragi itself.

However...

"Aren't those the precious points she's supposed to spend fighting superheroes and giant robots? The math doesn't make any sense."

"Yeah. Ammo sent from Earth is priced way higher than usual... She's probably thinking that using up all her points here and falling into the red isn't that terrible an outcome."

...Going back to Earth with a negative point balance means punishment, after all.

Seeing my puzzled expression, Alice gives a cheerful little shrug.

By now, the cords from the various weapons have all been plugged into Lilith.

The Demon Lord's Army, which has been warily keeping its distance, finally begins to move.

To be specific, Heine, their leader, starts walking toward us.

Once she's about twenty meters away, Heine calls out—

"Hey, Combat Agent Six. What are you doing out here? Are you up to one of your schemes again?"

Heine's already aware what's going on, and she smirks as she addresses us.

"Or is it that after drawing me away with your decoys, you were planning to go after His Lordship?"

...Damn, she's really onto us.

I mean, there's no other reason for us to be out here at the same time as Tiger Man's offensive.

"I still consider you a worthy opponent...which means if you want a fight, you're getting the whole army. Don't complain about fairness, okay? There's no other way to beat you and your machinations."

...Why is she taking the trouble of warning us?

"...But if you're willing to surrender so we can swap you for Russell in a hostage exchange, we'll consider listening."

Oh, I see. She hasn't given up on getting Russell back.

Unfortunately, it's much too late for him.

I mean, the fact that he's stopped objecting to dressing up like a girl among other things kinda makes it seem like he's already settled in, but it's more than that. He's learned the joys of having the Combat Agents depend on him to make their meals and do their laundry. He enjoys taking care of them in general.

Just then.

"Six, is that one of the leaders of the Demon Lord's Army?"

Her preparations complete, Lilith calls over to me.

"Yes, that's one of the Demon Lord's Elite Four, Heine of the Flames."

Hearing that, Lilith orders a PA speaker and calls out toward Heine—

"<Test, test. You, Boob Girl. Can you hear me?>"

Heine tilts her head at the sudden, booming voice calling out to her in Japanese, at which point, Lilith addresses them in the local language.

"We come bearing a message for the leadership of the Demon Lord's Army. We urge you to surrender to us. This is a warning. If you insist on fighting, in the name of Lilith the Black, this land will become a burning hellscape."

…Other than Heine, who looks a bit surprised at the ultimatum, the rest of the demons break out in raucous laughter.

While they hoot and holler, Heine, the only one not howling, slowly raises her hand. The laughter immediately stops.

"Since this is coming from your side, I doubt that threat is hollow. Six, who is that?"

Still on her guard, Heine calls over to me.

"This is my boss and one of our Supreme Leaders, Lady Lilith."

"O-one of your Supreme Leaders…"

Since she's already acknowledged us as fierce adversaries, this news causes Heine to break out in a cold sweat.

"Alice's example taught us not to underestimate anyone, not even a child. I mean, if she's this calm facing this giant army, there must be at least a speck of truth to those words."

The increasingly wary Heine once again waits for us to make the next move.

Seeing this, Lilith smiles faintly, as though things are moving as expected.

"…Well, what's it going to be, Heine of the Flames? Will you surrender? A fight will hurt my wallet, so I'd prefer a peaceful solution."

Lilith's casual attitude, indicating she doesn't much care which way things turn out, makes Heine even more cautious.

It's easy enough to see that Heine's seriously considering how to respond to Lilith and the mysterious weapons surrounding her.

"…We can't just back down to a handful of people. You sure you don't want to surrender? If you give us back Russell, we'll make sure to let you go… Your whole group's made up of young girls. Demons are pretty bloodthirsty. If a fight breaks out, I won't be able to stop 'em."

…Ah, it's come to threats.

But that's war for you.

We're an evil organization. We've seen plenty of awful scenes.

That's why I speak up next.

"Hear that, Alice? Heine's over there babbling nonsense about Lady Lilith surrendering. Seems she doesn't think much of Kisaragi, does she?"

As my words ring out across the wasteland, Heine's and (for some reason) Lilith's eyes widen in shock.

"Hah! They struggle enough with Six and me, yet they're going after Lady Lilith? They must have a death wish. If Lady Lilith wants to, she could easily vaporize everyone here in five seconds. I guess this is it for Heine. She might be our enemy, but I'll miss her..."

As Alice picks up the thread, Heine goes deathly pale.

...Is it just my imagination, or did Lilith do the same?

"W-wait! W-w-we're not disrespecting her...!"

"S-S-Six! Alice! I'm negotiating right now. Just hang on a minute."

Having come this far, I've made my peace with whatever happens.

Let's push it as far as it can go.

"Lady Lilith, leave it to me. We might not be much compared to your power, but we can at least stay out of the way and cover your back."

"And leave the support to me. If you end up hurt, I'll make sure to patch you up!"

Ignoring the panicking Lilith and Heine, we prep our weapons.

I have no idea what I can do against this giant army with just my R-Buzzsaw.

But...

"Lady Lilith can take out an army this size without breaking a sweat! Even if we lose, know that most of you aren't getting home alive!"

"Yeah, you guys are finished! Your opponent is Lilith the Black. There's a reason she's got the world's highest bounty on her head!"

As Alice and I shout out our challenges, the Demon Lord's Army stirs.

Responding to our aggressive posture, Heine calls out to us, shivering.

"Y-y-y-you're really going to do this?! F-f-f-f-fine! You're going to fight this army?! You're sure?! Absolutely sure?! I can't afford to have you disrespect me in front of my troops! I mean, it's a little late, given that I got sent to the castle in a compromising position thanks to Six, b-b-but I still can't afford it!"

"F-f-f-fine, let's do this! I can't show any weakness in front of my subordinates, either! Although, thanks to Six, my authority as a boss is pretty much wrecked."

The two of them exchange glances and, after a moment, let out sighs of relief—

"B-but, you know, we've already fought Tiger Man and suffered a lot of casualties. So maybe we'll pull back and call it a stalemate!"

"G-good point! Attacking you after Tiger Man's retreat would feel like I was just stealing his thunder! I couldn't do that! And no doubt we took a little damage ourselves, so we can let you go here..."

Keeping my R-Buzzsaw at the ready, I hurl an insult in support of Lilith at the Demon Lord's Army behind Heine.

"You pathetic bastards, you think you can disrespect Kisaragi and get away with it?! You losers are all dead meat! Alice, Rose, tell 'em!"

"Hah, they're not even worth killing. We'll capture you all and use you in my experiments!"

"A-as a Battle Chimera, fighting's in my blood! Lots of you look delicious! I'll go all out!"

I keep trash-talking as the two leaders look on with pale, shocked faces.

"We're the evil organization the Kisaragi Corporation! We're not afraid of some Demon Lord's Army or whatever! Come all at once, if you dare—!"

With support from her precious subordinates, Lilith also lets out a yell.

"Don't taunt them!"

5

Led by Heine, who's now braced for the worst, the Demon Lord's Army rushes toward us.

"Idiot! Six, you're an idiot! According to the reports, it's pretty clear Heine's afraid of you, so I thought we could get away with negotiations!"

"Eh, what are you talking about? You clearly weren't preparing to negotiate after making all these combat preparations."

Yes, Lilith, surrounded by heavy weaponry, is in her serious mode.

"This was to show I was serious and frighten them into submission! On Earth, most armies would surrender when I showed up like this! These weapons were just for show! I was trying to settle this peacefully so I can save my Evil Points!"

Oh, so that's what was going on.

Still…

"Lady Lilith, this isn't Earth, so they don't know about your serious mode."

"D-dammit!"

The distance between us and the Demon Lord's Army seems wide, but it isn't.

It probably won't take more than three minutes for them to charge across the wasteland to reach us.

Alice shouts some encouragement at Lilith as she fires shotgun rounds into the advancing infantry.

"Get ahold of yourself, Creator! You made me, so now show us what you're made of!"

"Alice, I have something to tell you later! Six is a meathead, so he might have misunderstood, but you taunted them while clearly knowing what I had in mind! Do you want to keep me on this planet that much, you needy little android?"

As she says this, Heine wreathes herself in flames and charges at Lilith.

"My easily provoked troops caused you some anxiety, huh? Sorry about that! I don't dislike kids, but if we beat you, we win! I won't hold back given the circumstances!"

"As leaders in evil organizations, we really do struggle with blood-thirsty subordinates, don't we? It's been a long time since someone said they won't hold back against me! I'm one of the most dangerous people on Earth, so it's been worth it just to hear you say that!"

Heine unleashes fireball after fireball as she approaches Lilith.

Seeing the weapons splayed around her target, Heine appears to have figured out that Lilith's a long-range fighter.

However—

"Eeep?! Wh-what the hell is this?!"

After having all her fireballs deflected by Lilith's tentacles, Heine finds herself constricted in no time at all.

"Mwa-ha-ha-ha-ha-ha-ha! Inflicting perverted situations on people is part of a female evil Supreme Leader's job description! Look, Six! The tentacle punishment!"

"Well done, Lady Lilith! You know how Combat Agents think! So you're gonna strip Heine naked in front of her troops, right?"

"S-stop!"

"Can you two actually do a bit of work? Why is the Combat Agent Recruit doing all the fighting?"

Prompted to glance at the front line by Alice's criticism, I see Rose breathing fire to push back the approaching horde.

"Wow, she really can breathe fire! Alice, if we can take her back to Earth—"

"You're going to say she'll be a clean and eco-friendly energy source, right? I figured that out when I met her! Hurry up and show us your serious mode, Creator!"

I repel an orc attacking Alice with my R-Buzzsaw and call out to Rose.

"Rose! Fall back a second! Lady Lilith's about to show her serious mode!"

"What?! I didn't say a single thing about... Oh, for crying out loud!"

After Rose takes a big leap backward, Heine, who's been tangled in the tentacles, is tossed toward her troops.

"Ahhhhhhhh?! Y-you...!"

Landing on the ground with a thud, Heine tries to get a barb in...

...but the now-unencumbered tentacles are all pointing at the Demon Lord's Army—

"Whaaaaaaaa—?! W-wait! Hold...!"

Heine, who rolled headfirst through the dirt, lets out a confused wail as a sudden storm of explosions and shock waves rains down around her.

Stunned, she watches countless bullets, shells, lightning, and heat rays scatter the Demon Lord's Army.

"Waaaaahooo! Run, little piggies, RUN! This is the power of the Kisaragi Corporation! Watch and learn!"

"This is what happens when you diss my creator!"

"Boss, Miss Alice, let's not shout from behind Lady Lilith."

Several of the soldiers shoot arrows and spells at the little scientist, but her tentacles stop them all...

"Wh-what the hell is this?! F-f-fa...fall back! ALL OF YOU, FALL BACK!"

Heine screams while sprawled on the ground, but Lilith, her eyes bloodshot in concentration, shouts over her.

"This is your final warning! This is only ten percent of my true power. You think that's just a bluff? Those words are going to jinx me? Fine. Then let me show you!"

The Demon Lord's Army, Heine included, must have caught sight of the black objects suddenly blinking into existence above them.

Seems most of the teleported weapons were for show, but the satellite uplink is real.

No doubt she connected her brain directly to the satellite, setting the sky overhead as the coordinates.

The antipersonnel cluster munitions, which were teleported from Kisaragi headquarters, hurtle toward the ground—

"Next, I'll bombard your army! If I do, you'll no doubt get desperate and fight to the last man! I repeat! This is your final warning! ...If my points hit the negatives because of you lot, I'm staying on this planet! I don't care either way! I'm perfectly happy enjoying life here with Six, Alice, and Rose."

Before she can finish her warning, countless explosions go off in a deafening typhoon of sound, kicking up an enormous dust storm in the process.

6

The full-scale war with the Demon Lord's Army—or rather, the one-sided massacre by a single Supreme Leader—comes to an end.

Thanks to Heine's quick surrender, there weren't too many deaths, and our self-proclaimed medic, Alice, has tended to most of the wounded, leaving the recovering demons to rest in a single spot.

And in front of Lilith...

"Lady Lilith, we've brought one of the Elite Four, Heine of the Flames."

"Keep walking, you damn heifer. You want those tits ripped off?"

"E-eeep! S-stop...please..."

With Alice and me grabbing her from either side, Heine, after her complete surrender, is dragged to face the music.

"What'll we do with her, Lady Lilith? This Heine of the Flames, one of the Demon Lord's Elite Four, has gone around causing all sorts of trouble for me. This bitch always finds a way to create new headaches."

"Yeah, she keeps showing up and bullying us."

"What?! Wait, I don't remember doing anything like that...! I mean, sure, I've tried to foil your plots, but it's more that you've been victimizing us...!"

Forced to her knees before Lilith, Heine pleads in her own defense as Alice and I rat her out.

Seeing our behavior...

"...You know. You two have gotten worse by the day since you got here."

"I just take after my boss."

"I take after my creator."

Lilith purses her lips in frustration at the immediacy of our response.

"So what'll we do with her, Lady Lilith? We gonna court-martial her? I demand she be sentenced to three years of titty torture."

"I think we should make her work like a dog as a bottom-tier Combat Agent."

Heine begins shuddering at our proposals.

"I'm not going to conduct a court-martial. Yes, the Kisaragi Corporation is in direct opposition to the Demon Lord's Army, but only as a private military contractor that's deploying our Combat Agents to the Grace Kingdom. We're basically mercenaries. It's the Grace Kingdom that's at war with the Demon Lord's Army, which means we have no right to punish her."

As Lilith sighs, Heine blinks in confusion.

After a moment, it seems a faint spark of hope is starting to glow in her chest...

"Wow, that's pretty awful, Lady Lilith. So you're saying she won't even get the minimum rights guaranteed to her during the trial, huh? That's great."

"Damn, that's impressively evil, Lady Lilith. Model behavior for an evil organization's Supreme Leader."

"Hold on, that's not what I said! I have no intention of doing anything like that! Don't look so scared! You don't have to listen to these two!"

Lilith quickly reassures Heine, who sinks into the pits of despair.

"I can't quite let you go yet, but I don't mind releasing you once you answer a few questions. In fact, depending on the information, I'll even listen to a couple of your requests."

"...?! R-really?! Th-then, while I know I'm being presumptuous..."

Heine looks toward her wounded troops...

"Um, could you move your Chimera away from the wounded soldiers...?"

"Hey! What are you doing over there?! I told you not to eat the bodies of monsters that can speak human languages, but you also can't eat the ones that are still alive, either!"

We already warned Rose not to eat the dead demons, but...

"I-I'll make sure to drive that point home later. Anyway, there were a few things I wanted to ask you..."

*   *   *

"Ways to get into the Demon Lord's Castle?"

"Yes, that's right. You need to gather some sort of item to get into the Demon Lord's Castle, right?"

Lilith is asking Heine how to either slip into the Demon Lord's Castle or remove the barrier protecting it.

"...Um, well, if you put the sorcerer stones, otherwise known as 'release keys,' into the towers to the north, south, east, and west of the castle..."

"We already know about that method. The problem is we can't gather all those sorcerer stones or whatever they're called."

We're out of luck if there's no way in without them.

In which case, Lilith will either blast it with massive amounts of explosives or take the entire Demon Lord's Kingdom hostage and demand that the barrier be dropped.

"...From what I've heard, the sorcerer stones have the effect of suspending the protective features of the towers. Which means if you can destroy the towers themselves, they can't protect the castle. Of course, destroying towers is a ridiculous idea..."

"Oh, I see. Well, it wouldn't be hard for me to destroy a few towers."

Huh, that was quickly sorted.

"B-but a particularly thick fog shrouds each of the towers, hiding them. You can't remove those mists without using the treasure from the Tower of Duster. O-oh, and I only know the location of the Flame Tower! Th-that's the truth! I swear!"

"...Hey, Alice, didn't we hand over the treasure from the Tower of Duster to the kingdom?"

"Yeah, the missing Chosen One had it on him. Which means the treasure's missing, too."

How useless. The Chosen One is completely useless.

Lilith speaks up suddenly.

"Well, in that case, there's an easy solution."

Sounds like she's thought of something.

"What is it, Lady Lilith? A giant fan? We're gonna blow away the fog with a giant fan and find the towers?"

"Why would we bother with something like that? No, the four towers are always covered by fog, right? Then the answer is simple."

Lilith says this as though stating the obvious, and a particularly evil smile plays on her lips.

7

"Heine, you're absolutely sure, right? None of your kingdom's people live near the towers, right? Because if you're wrong, it's your ass on the line, even if she's the one wiping out your civilians."

"It's true! I wouldn't lie in the face of that sort of power! I mean, are you people sane? Destroying entire areas covered by fog to destroy the towers?! What sort of insane tactic is that?!"

Lilith's plan involves specifically targeting locations where the fog is thickest and bombing the hell out of them.

Alice has already linked with the satellite and found these locations.

"She's right. There are spots in the north, south, east, and west with heavy concentrations of fog."

"Looking at it from above, they're just marking where the towers are."

The mad scientist and her creation are happily taking notes on the coordinates.

"Ohhh... What a terrible day... The moment she sends a piece of paper somewhere, those things from earlier will rain down on them...

This is a nightmare... This is a day of reckoning for demons... The moment the barrier drops, you're going to bombard the Demon Lord's Castle, right? This kingdom is doomed..."

As Heine breaks down in tears, I tell her:

"No, we're not gonna bomb the castle. See our Chimera over there? She's got a few things she wants to ask your Demon Lord. Which is why we're here to talk to him."

Heine's eyes widen, staring at me as if I said something particularly egregious, at which point she proceeds to berate me.

"A t-talk?! Did you just say you wanted to talk?! You did all this just for a chat?! All that taunting and destruction just to have a conversation?! I'm going to kill you! You're going to join my dead soldiers!"

"Oh? You're gonna kill me? You? The loser? You understand you're a prisoner, right? Also, I'm going to hell when I die, so you just admitted your soldiers are in hell, too!"

Just as Heine and I start fighting...

A loud explosion rings out from the distance, and shortly thereafter, the ground beneath us quakes.

I look over to see Lilith and Alice have finished their calculations.

"Shit, you really did it... I mean, if all you wanted to do was talk, we could've negotiated... Why do you lunatics always resort to brute force...?"

Well, I mean, we are an evil organization, after all.

"Hey, Rose, over here. Come."

"......?"

Following sincere discussion among Heine, Lilith, and myself...

"Rose, Heine's going to talk to the Demon Lord and show you around the ruins in the Demon Lord's Castle. Then, she's going to arrange a talk with the Demon Lord for you. Of course, on our end, we've also got a proposal to just charge into the castle and extract the information by force."

Rose responds without missing a beat.

"Let's go with talking! Talking, please!"

Rose's reaction transforms Heine's expression from being on the verge of tears to suggesting she's found a ray of hope.

For the record, there are three votes to skip the talking and just storm the castle.

Which means everyone other than Rose prefers to just settle the matter now, but…

"Are you sure? There's the possibility they won't keep their word, and we don't know when it'll actually happen. I mean, we've still got Lady Lilith with us, so we can probably end it today."

Rose shakes her head at my whispered suggestion.

"…No, I would rather have a peaceful chat. But, Boss, it's thanks to you, Miss Alice, and Lady Lilith that we've come this far, so that's just my vote. I can't insist too much, but…"

"…I see. Well, in that case, let's do it your way. According to our company's Kisaragi System, the concerned party's preference is worth a hundred votes."

Lilith's remark settles our policy from here on out.

Heine lets out a deep sigh of relief, and Rose blushes happily.

Lady Lilith, I've never heard of this Kisaragi System.

"All right then, Six. Let's head back to the hideout. My brain got a hell of a workout today, so I'm going to gorge myself on sweets. Also, we need to write up a report. You two need to sing my praises in yours, okay? Like stuff about how I defeated the Demon Lord's Army with one finger, how I knocked out a dragon with a single punch…"

"……"

I let myself think she'd lied for Rose's sake, but I'm starting to suspect she just wants to get home as quickly as possible.

8

"What do you mean? You did all that?! Why didn't you call on me for such an important mission?!"

It's the day after our blitzkrieg against the Demon Lord's Army.

I'm taking the brunt of Grimm's ire as, after hearing the news, she's come to the hideout to complain.

"Bwaaaaaaaaaaaaaaaaaah! *Sniff, sob...* Bwaaaaaaaaaaaaaaaaaah!"

......

"I thought we were family, Commander. Why did you exclude me?! I mean, Rose and I are best friends!"

"Well, that's because we decided the whole thing late at night. Also, I don't know where you live. Besides, we executed the operation in the early morning. You're totally not a morning person."

"I would've given you my address if you'd just asked! Also, if it was for Rose, I would've done a morning op!"

"Bwaaah! *Sob, sob...* Waaaaaaaah!"

....

Grimm wasn't the only one who charged in.

A conspicuously dirty Snow is sprawled on the ground, weeping uncontrollably and making a mess of our brand-new floors with her tears.

"...Commander, can't you do anything about that?"

"What am I supposed to do, exactly? I tried to tell her, but I couldn't find her anywhere inside the city. And then when it comes down to it..."

This sinfully greedy woman had been relentlessly assailing the Sky King's lair since the day it kidnapped me, plotting to steal treasure.

...Yes, the silhouette we saw being chased by the Sky King on our way to the Demon Lord's Castle was Snow.

Now that she's heard we put up remarkable results by rampaging against the Demon Lord's Army in her absence, Snow has been reduced to an inconsolable mess.

Feeling sympathetic, Rose approaches Snow and gently pats her head while wiping her face.

"...I know it wasn't for long, but she was your commander for a while, right? She's only in the way here, so can't you just drag her back to the city?"

"I'd prefer not to. I mean, she doesn't have a place to stay right now. Am I supposed to just leave her on the roadside? I can't do that to her. And my place is single occupancy..."

You know, Snow's more trouble than she's worth. I'm just gonna wait until she exhausts herself and falls asleep.

I have more important business to take care of anyway.

Summoned by Lilith, I make my way to the hideout's teleporter room.

"Hey, Six, I've been waiting on you."

Having finished the final adjustments to the teleporter and tested the link to Kisaragi headquarters, Lilith stands in front of the glass pod of the device, a giant backpack on her shoulders.

"Seems you were getting quite an earful. Though, if you'd done the same to me, I probably wouldn't have let you off that easy. Be sure you make it up to them later."

"I mean, I've got legit reasons this time. One of them is nocturnal and refuses to walk despite being fully capable, and the other wasn't even in the city at the time."

As I rattle off the excuses, Lilith smiles faintly in amusement.

"For my part, I still don't understand those two very well, and they're more like enemies than friends, but whatever. You have my permission to keep them close to you for now."

"If I need permission to keep women close to me, why don't you take a page out of their book and do the same?"

I say it teasingly, eliciting a smirk from Lilith.

"Oh really? In that case, I can stay here for you. But I know the moment I try to do that you'll... Never mind, I got it wrong again. You're not that sort of person. I'm really sorry. It's not like that. I just wanted to tease you every now and then! You know, like in a romance light novel!"

I lumber toward her with my arms outstretched, and Lilith scrambles backward, rambling.

What a coward... One of these days, she's gonna push me too far.

"What's with that look? That's not how you should look at your boss! Alice, Aliiice! Come here!"

Alice, who's been running a diagnostic on the teleporter, comes over at Lilith's insistence.

"It's almost time, and you're still flirting...? What do you need?"

"...It's time to start the actual conquest, but Six is soft. I'm worried he might let his ties to the locals affect his judgment, which is why I plan to give you some broad orders for the foreseeable future."

I mean, Lilith also let her fondness for the locals affect her judgment.

Lilith flips from relaxed to stern, her hand on her hip and her tone serious.

"Attention!"

Alice and I straighten, standing at attention.

"Combat Agent Six, pretty-girl android Alice Kisaragi. You two are to begin espionage and invasion preparations on the surrounding kingdoms, using this hideout as your base. In parallel, you will be responsible for founding a city capable of supporting human life in this area, with this fortress at its center. Bring life back to these wastelands, tame those woods, and create a foundation for settling earthlings on this planet!"

......

"Lady Lilith, can I ask a question?"

"I'm still in the middle of explaining...but whatever, go ahead."

Lilith's tone suggests she expects this sort of thing from me.

"I understand the part about espionage and invasion preparations on the surrounding kingdoms. I mean, we've already put enough points on the board that I think Alice and I should be allowed to go home, but still."

Heading home with my Evil Points still in the red would end badly, so I put that aside.

...Besides, I've grown kind of fond of this place.

"The part I don't understand is the city-building. What's with giving us a mission that sounds like it requires serious brainpower? I don't like saying it myself, but I'm not very smart. I have no confidence I'd be able to do anything like politics or governing."

Lilith nods as if already aware of this.

"I know better than anyone that you're a meathead. I don't expect you're capable of any decent city-building."

You know, despite the fact that I won't see her for a while, she's still getting her barbs in.

"The city's mayor will be Alice Kisaragi. As Alice's partner, you'll be responsible for taking care of the dirty work. We're building a metropolis from scratch in a place like this. There are bound to be problems of one sort or another, like conflicts with the neighboring kingdoms and the savages and monsters from the woods. Once the city's founded and the population grows, there'll be crime to worry about. Obviously, criminal organizations other than our own will try to muscle in. Your job is to resolve those problems using force."

...Oh, so the usual, then.

"Six, do you play any simulation games? You know, like RTS or nation-building games? The sort where you gather resources, build a base, then slowly expand your territory by defeating things like monsters around you?"

"To be honest, I only really play porn games."

"O-oh, I see. Well then, never mind. At any rate…make sure we put down roots in this clean, green world that, as of yet, remains unspoiled by radiation or chemicals! Fortunately, there's a lot of undeveloped land. Start working these unclaimed territories, and for places that are already settled, conquer them after thoroughly investigating them!"

Alice and I snap off the Combat Agent salute in acknowledgment of our orders.

Seeing our reaction, Lilith smiles happily.

"I'm counting on you two. So I'm going to go home…but don't put all your focus on this planet. Think of the three of us back on Earth from time to time."

As she enters the pod, Lilith glances away shyly.

"Well, see ya later, Lady Lilith. I thought you were pretty useless when you first got here, but you rallied at the end. Make sure you live in a manner worthy of being my creator."

"Hey, who's the parent here? But sure, I'll aim to be a parent you can be proud of."

I suddenly remember something when I see Lady Lilith's blushing face.

"Lady Lilith. There was something I needed to tell you as well. You interrupted me on the roof before I could."

Yes, it had been when Lilith was half crying, telling me not to forget them.

I'd been preparing to say the following:

"Not a day goes by that I've forgotten you three. Because…"

With the backpack on her back, Lilith fidgets more than usual, her cheeks flushed bright red.

"…I think about all of you every night! I wanted to make sure you knew that! As for why I think about the three of you at night, well, even porn costs Evil Points, so…"

"Wow! That's really awful! You're really awful! Don't you dare

come back to Earth! I'm going to tell Astaroth and Belial about this!
You better remember this! You damned pervert of a subordinate!"

Seems our beloved boss was hoping for something different…

With that last line, she smiles faintly to herself as she disappears
into the teleporter—

In the room housing the giant teleporter at the Kisaragi Corporation's headquarters.

Usually, a small group of administrative staff would be on hand to fulfill resource requests from agents dispatched to the corners of this world and beyond. Today, though, the atmosphere is different.

Two of the Supreme Leaders of the organization wait impatiently for their colleague, Lilith the Black, to return from her assignment on the alien planet, temporarily code-named Second Earth.

Electricity suddenly sparks through the teleporter's glass booth.

Then, with neither a glittering magic circle nor a bright flash of light...

...Lilith appears in front of her colleagues, a backpack on her shoulders and a happy smile on her face.

Catching a glimpse of the two, Lilith makes no attempt to conceal her good mood, practically skipping as she exits the teleporter.

"Hey, guys, I'm back! Wow, coming to welcome me home, huh? Tsk, don't you two have work you should be doing? Well, but I suppose we've known one another since we founded this enterprise, and this was the first time we've been apart so long... I guess we can let that go just this once!"

Completely misreading the room, Lilith breezily unslings her pack, dropping it with a *thud* to the floor.

"Ta-daa! See what I've got here? Jewels and gold coins from the other side. You know, when I first met her, I thought she was an evil, scheming bitch of a royal, but Princess Tillis of Grace is a brilliant leader! When she realized just how much I'd accomplished, she piled up the rewards for me. Not to sound like Six, but it almost makes me want to go native!"

Oblivious to Astaroth's chilly gaze, Lilith continues droning on.

"It's such a pity you guys missed my performance. Have you read Six and Alice's reports yet? I actually wanted to discuss them with you..."

"Lilith."

Astaroth's sudden interruption locks Lilith in place, the little scientist failing to suppress an involuntary shudder.

"...U-um, yes? Wh-what's with the look? Y-you're starting to scare me a little. Wh-while you're at it, could you cut it out with the freezing? It's creepy, and it's getting really, really cold..."

Lilith backs away fearfully, shielding the pack behind her back.

...Belial chooses that moment to approach, wrapping her arm around the cowering Lilith's shoulder.

"Welcome home, Lilith. You really enjoyed yourself over there, mm?"

"Hey, Belial! Yep, it was a lot of fun! First thing I ran into over there was this giant lizard. It was no match for me, of course! And THEN it turns out that lizard's lair was this ancient ruin, and... O-ow! That's hot!"

A sharp cry of pain erupts from Lilith midspiel.

Belial's bright-red hair ripples like flame, as though expressing her current frame of mind.

Lilith tries to peel Belial's hand off her shoulder but is thwarted by the unexpected strength of her comrade's grip.

"H-hey, Belial, this is getting a little stuffy! Did you miss me that much?! I've heard of warm welcomes, but this is way over the top! It's sweltering... Ow! That's way too hot! You're going to burn me! Step off... Dammit, get away from me!"

Reaching her limit, Lilith tries to use her tentacles to get some distance, but Belial calmly steps away.

Astaroth chuckles drily watching Lilith's antics.

"Heh. Now, now, Lilith, you just can't seem to stay still, can you? Complaining about the cold, then the heat. Can't make up your mind?"

"Room temperature would be great! Just normal room temperature, please! What the hell's gotten into you two? Why are you in such a pissy mood?!"

Astaroth, her lips quirked in a creepily thin smile, slowly closes her eyes.

"Surely, you can figure that out on your own. Place your hand against that flat little chest of yours and think carefully."

Lilith responds by doing exactly as suggested, placing her palm against her chest.

"...The only thing that comes to mind is that my breasts are perfectly shaped and proportionate—a work of art, even..."

"Yo, Astaroth, looks like she's not getting it."

"Indeed. In fact, she seems quite smug."

Lilith's comeback appears to have flipped a switch in her sister Supreme Leaders.

"Wh-what? What the hell is wrong with you guys...?! ...Aha! I got it. Souvenirs. You want your souvenirs, right? Oh, you're so materialistic. Just so we're clear, I *earned* all this with my hard work, so I'm doing you two a favor by splitting it with you, okay? Just make sure you show me some respect."

With that, Lilith softly places a single jewel into each of their hands.

...And in the blink of an eye, the blue gem in Astaroth's palm is coated in frost before shattering, while the red jewel in Belial's hand is engulfed in flame, melting away.

"Why'd you do that?! You saw the colors of those gems, right? I chose those two specifically because they were your favorite colors! How could you?! This is how you repay me for all my efforts over there? Now I'm upset! Get lost; I don't want to see your faces today! I mean, sure, those were cheap rocks I was planning to toss, but still! Now I'm just going to…"

…*head home.*

The words die in Lilith's mouth as Astaroth and Belial grab her shoulders, holding her in place.

"Souvenirs and jewels are irrelevant. So I'll ask one more time, Lilith. What exactly did you get up to over there? Did you *enjoy yourself*?"

"Of course I did! I'm sorry, okay? You're upset I got to have Six to myself for a while, right? But you're blaming the wrong person. After all, Six is the one who picked me out of us three, remember?"

Astaroth's eyebrow twitches as Lilith needlessly pours oil on the fire.

"Oh, don't be silly, Lilith. I wouldn't be angry about such a petty thing."

"For real? I remember watching your brow twitch each time Alice sent a video of Six and Lilith having fun."

"Oh, don't be silly, Lilith. I wouldn't be angry about such a petty thing."

Pretending not to hear Belial, Astaroth repeats herself.

"You forgot what you were sent over there to do, didn't you?"

…The room goes silent at the accusation.

"…Whoa, whoa, hold on, Astaroth. What's that supposed to mean? I made a big splash over there. I fought all sorts of monsters, like the lord of the ancient ruins guarding the Cursed Forest, and this bothersome creature called the Mud King, and even the grand Lord of the Skies… And of course, at the end, confronting our competitors, I…"

"You came home without finishing off the competition."

…

"You've got it all wrong."

"These reports say you fought a giant lizard, a ball of slime, and a sparrow, then shut yourself in after a pretty cosplayer scared the crap out of you."

Lilith's expression freezes as Belial reads off a sheet of paper.

"That's not true! Well, okay, that's pretty much true, but it's wrong! The giant lizard was actually a huge robot, and the blob of slime was big enough to fill up the entire space beneath the country! And while fighting a sparrow sounds ridiculous, it was really, really big! In fact, it's a sparrow that feeds on monsters in the sky! It wasn't your average, everyday sparrow. It's a really impressive specimen that rivaled the pet I used to keep! And that wasn't a cosplayer; she was an angel! An ANGEL! You could tell she was trouble from a single glance! And I didn't run away and come home…"

Sensing she's in trouble, Lilith starts vomiting up excuses at a rapid clip.

In response, Belial produces another sheet of paper and begins reading.

"…It says here you stared at a cross-dresser's penis?"

"…I mean, if I had to say whether I did or not, then yes, I did, but so what?! I thought he was the female Chimera from the reports! But he turned out to be a boy!"

Lilith puts up a thin defense, prompting the pair to render judgment in unison:

""Guilty.""

At that, Lilith pushes away the hands on her shoulders, clutching the bag she'd been shielding against her chest to make her escape…!

"Blocked!"

Spouting a line from a popular RPG, Belial quickly obstructs Lilith's path.

Seeing her escape thwarted, Lilith's face twitches into a grimace, as a smiling Astaroth quickly approaches from behind…

"Your mission was to crush the competition and bring Six home. No one sent you over there to go sightseeing. And these souvenirs? You're just trying to win us over after failing your primary objective."

"Heh-heh, hand over the goods, little girl. Oh? Think you're making it out of here? Tch, taking a vacation and leaving all the work to us... Your cheeks are all smooth!"

Belial to the front of her. Astaroth to the back of her.

Surrounded by Kisaragi's Supreme Leaders, the useless one of their number, who still has a faint whiff of naïveté to her, stands staring into the mouth of death...

"D-damn you! Trying to rob me of my hard-earned loot on a technicality?! How evil! I'm impressed! ...But c'mon, admit it; you're both just jealous. You're jealous of the fact that Six likes me and chose me out of all of us! Yeah, I'll admit it! I had all sorts of fun over there with Six! We explored a mysterious new world and had a blast doing it! If you miss Six that much, you ought to be more honest with yourselves and go see him! If you want this treasure, you'll have to act like proper villains and take it from me! Jerks! Dummies!"

As Lilith abandons any pretense and fires back, the veins on Astaroth's and Belial's foreheads bulge into view.

Lilith wraps her arms in a death grip around her backpack, then unleashes all her tentacles...!

"Come at me, you villains! I'm Lilith the Black, Scourge of the Demon Lord!!"

Lilith's cry echoes throughout the halls of the Kisaragi Corporation's headquarters.

AFTERWORD

Thank you so much for picking up this fourth volume of *Combatants Will Be Dispatched!*

With four volumes, there are now enough pages that if you layer them together in your shirt, you could use them in lieu of a bulletproof vest. And it's all thanks to you, dear reader.

I've been thinking that it's pretty impressive for someone as easily distracted as I am to keep working on something, whether we're talking about *Konosuba* or *Combatants*. Thinking on it further, I realized this is the first time I've held a job for five straight years.

Hey now, no need to look at me like I'm a failure of a human being.

In the hopes that *Combatants* will become a long-running series, let's spend a little time talking about it.

As I mentioned in the first volume, the end goal of the series isn't to kill the Demon Lord.

Instead, the objective is to invade a new alien planet to provide a refuge for humanity as Earth nears its various limits.

The main character in this series has a big responsibility, just as the main character in the conventional *isekai* adventure-fantasy series *Konosuba* is tasked with saving humanity from the Demon King.

Will he act for the good of humanity and Kisaragi and complete the conquest of this new world? Or will he finally tire of the constant bait-and-switches and turn around to protect his new subordinates from his old bosses?

The planet itself is still largely unexplored and full of mysteries.

As we move forward, the adventures continue as our heroes build a giant metropolis using the power of technology and solve the mysteries of this world!

But remember: Fundamentally, this is still a comedy, so don't invest *too* heavily in that premise.

If you'd like to read a proper adventuring story, I'll go ahead and recommend you pick up my other series, *Konosuba*.

The movie should be out around the time this volume is released, so I hope you can enjoy that serious trailer along with the movie.

At any rate, like last time, I was able to release this volume thanks to the efforts of others.

I'd like to close with my usual remarks, along with thanks and apologies to Kakao Lanthanum, the illustrator; my project manager K, my editors, the designers, and the sales team, along with all the other people who pitched in to get this book out the door.

And to all the readers who've taken the time to pick up this volume, you have my deep, deep thanks!

Natsume Akatsuki